A Woman of
Five Seasons

A Woman of
Five Seasons

BY LEILA AL-ATRASH

Translated by N. Halwani & C. Tingley

Interlink Books
An imprint of Interlink Publishing Group, Inc.
New York • Northampton

For Dana and Tamim and Mada

First published in 2002 by
INTERLINK BOOKS
An imprint of Interlink Publishing Group, Inc.
99 Seventh Avenue • Brooklyn, New York 11215 and
46 Crosby Street • Northampton, Massachusetts 01060
www.interlinkbooks.com

Original Arabic copyright © by Leila al-Atrash 1990, 2002
English translation copyright © by Salma Khadra Jayyusi 2002

Originally published in Arabic as *Imra'at al-Fousool al-Khamsa* by Al-Mouassasa
al-Arabiyya Lil Dirasat Wal Nashr, Beirut, 1990.
This translation was prepared by PROTA, Project of Translation from Arabic
Literature, founded and directed by Salma Khadra Jayyusi.

Library of Congress Cataloging-in-Publication Data

Al-Atrash, Leila
  [Imra'at al-fousool al-khamsah. English]
 A woman of five seasons / by Leila Al-Atrash ; translated by Nora
Nweihid Halwani and Christopher Tingley.
    p. cm. — (Emerging voices)
  ISBN 1-56656-416-6
  I. Halwani, Nora Nweihid. II. Tingley, Christopher. III. Title.
IV. Series.
PJ7814.T72 I47 2001
892.7'36—dc21

                                    2001006203

Printed and bound in Canada by Webcom Ltd.

Cover painting by Suha Shoman, courtesy of The Royal Society of Fine Art, Jordan
National Gallery of Fine Arts, Amman, Jordan.

To request our complete 40-page full-color catalog,
please call us toll free at **1-800-238-LINK,** visit our
website at **www.interlinkbooks.com**, or write to
Interlink Publishing
46 Crosby Street, Northampton, MA 01060
e-mail: info@interlinkbooks.com

CONTENTS

ONE

Soles of the Feet

"My lovely kitten—this perfume suits you better."
He was trying to say something, trying to make
her say something. Anything to wake her up and get her to
talk. But her face was still without expression, and, in spite
of himself, he started to feel upset, a hint of anger rising
inside him. He tried to curb his desire, to force her awake.
He gazed at her features, taking pleasure, as he always did,
in the sight of her stilled by a deep inner relaxation that left
her body motionless.

Thrusting his arm under her head, he lifted her up,
feeling a slight prickling as his skin touched her bare back
and their sweat mingled. She remained asleep.

Letting go of her, he lit a cigarette. He gazed reflectively at
the elegant silver box, read the name of the international
company on the gold lighter, then deliberately let it clatter
on the bedside table, but no sound whatever came from her.

"I'm half choking," he said irritably. "This air conditioner
doesn't work."

The desire to wake her was too much for him. As she lay
there still, he started muttering. Her eyes remained closed,
but words came slowly from between her lips: "I set it at
sixty degrees."

1

"Are you trying to stifle me? I'm not going out to change the setting. This heat's unbearable, it's killing me. Have a bit of pity!"

As the bathroom door slammed behind him, the tension raced through his veins. He cocked his ears to hear if she was turning there on the bed, but no sound came. He made a deliberate noise, moved everything he touched, hoping to wake her. He turned the tap on violently, and the shower jetted strong and hot, recalling the blazing day just past.

He let the water tickle his body, washing him with its hot jet. After a few moments, he didn't know how many, he felt his smile growing ever broader. If only she'd wake and come to him! Still, the day lay ahead, awaiting both of them, and she looked more beautiful when she was rested. Once more he felt a need for her, with all his mind and instincts, but he resisted the desire.

When she'd slept, she always rose with a clear complexion and radiant eyes. She looked prettier when those wild tresses of hers circled her full face, when her cheeks had become rosy like those of a chubby child. He fought back a clamorous laugh, which came out, finally, as a brief, cut-off chuckle: "Her tresses!"

A surge of forgiveness swept through him, for her deception. Shaking his head, he started massaging his body with liquid soap that sent out a heady fragrance, mingled with the steam. He poured some shampoo on his hair, then cursed out loud as he remembered he'd washed it just the afternoon before. He rubbed it, and felt how its smoothness started to sink into the creeping roughness of the strands he'd flattened earlier with the dryer.

What an idiot you were, Ihsan, he thought. For years you were taken in by the smoothness of her hair! That smoothness never stopped inflaming your palms. You saw it there in her hair, felt it in the silken touch, while your mind magnified its wonder—making the tresses fly and flirt with your face! You trembled each time she raised her face to you. Bewitching—with the silken threads encircling that round, child-like face of hers. You never dreamed, for a moment even, that its texture might change. For years it went on exciting you—you couldn't sleep because of it—the silk teasing your face—tickling the nakedness of your dreams! And when you married her, her hair was bewitching, soft and straight. Then you went off, and your only thought was of her joining you, for she, and her hair, to become yours alone!

But those new projects, all that endless business in Barqais, stopped you from going back to fetch her. That was right and proper, so your mother told you, and Faris agreed. And so Nadia came by herself, in a lovely rosy dress, her soft hair awaiting the thrusts of your fingers.

God, how didn't you see it? Her face, desperately pleading—her frightened eyes, as she fought your desire to be with her, for the first time, beneath the water! Her fear, her virginal shyness overruling you. You'd dreamed so long of a moment like that—and she screamed! You didn't know which part of her body she was hiding as you dragged her into the water. How didn't you see it?

You'd dreamed, for so long, of walking with her in the rain, your arms around her, her soaked clothes clinging to her body, the raindrops sprinkling from the threads of her soft, cascading hair—and that dream never came true.

From the first time she agreed to meet you, before you asked for her hand and after, her hair was always smooth. She took you in! She didn't once think of letting it keep its natural shape, so you'd know her as she is.

As you waited for her to arrive, the sky darkened suddenly. The armies of clouds were being beaten along by the wind, and the people on foot hurried off out of the rain, leaving the street almost empty. Lightning split the blackness of the sky, lit it up, then the thunder cracked. You waited for her happily, wanted to enfold her—hide her and protect her from the rain, inside your jacket! You'd take it off, you decided, and wrap it gallantly around her shoulders, the way heroes do in the movies. It was past four o'clock— at five Nadia still hadn't come. You gave her until five-thirty, but she never arrived.

Darkness crept over the streets, and you were showered with dirty water splashed from the passing cars. Those drivers rev right up when they see someone standing in a storm, just to rub it in—that you don't have a car and dry clothes like them.

You walked up and down the street several times, looking for shelter under the shop awnings, avoiding the puddles and the water rushing toward the mouths of the drains. You didn't lose your hope that she'd come. Your dream, of embracing her damp body, gave you strength, helped you to endure.

At seven the shops started closing. You waited on, until no one was left there but you. But she didn't come! And when you scolded her, she just said, coquettishly: "I don't like being out in the rain."

Was that why, Ihsan, you carried her off to the shower the day she arrived? She started crying out, shyly trying to hide the parts of her body you were laying bare. Then, suddenly, she forgot everything! Her hands moved to protect her hair from the shower that was streaming down; her tresses snaked back, then grew shorter. The shock of her curly hair took you aback. But you forgave all that the moment you carried her off to bed and she became your woman.

She was still dozing, some sweat on her tired brow. Her breathing had grown regular. As he lay down beside her, he deliberately tucked up her body, leaning over to take the art magazine from the bedside table. She didn't stir.

She talked well, and lately she'd started talking cleverly about fashions and artists. She didn't even insist so much, now, on having books. He was well content with her new hobby.

Tomorrow, he thought, will Nadia be able to stand out? Make other women say how elegant she is? Will she know how to use her fingers and neck, to make the diamonds shine on them?

And if she does? Then, Ihsan, those women will talk about your wife to their husbands—and the men will talk about you! Barqais will come to know just what Ihsan Natour's worth!

That other diamond was quite a big one, surrounded by fair-sized rubies—rare and precious, handed down to your mother by her grandmother. It didn't have the glitter skilled polishing gives jewelry today. But that sad glint in your mother's eyes was bright enough, as she handed it to you, then hurried off to the kitchen.

You had to sell it! There was pleading in her eyes as she handed it over. But you had no other choice.

He'd hated his fear that she really would cling on to it, despised his foreboding as he cunningly implored her to keep it. He'd loathed his resentment of her weakness and feared she'd keep it after all, on account of his insistence and her memories of the jealousy it aroused, when she wore it, among the women she knew.

It was her last piece of jewelry, and she'd known how to

wear it to good effect, to show it off. It was the last of what she'd kept! She'd started selling her gold, piece by piece; and, as his father's illness went on, there were ever fewer pieces with diamonds and other gems in the small box she hid in the bottom of her wooden closet.

That ring had been all that was left when her husband passed away. His father had called him and his brother Jalal. The veins stood out feebly in his hands, his body, once so tall, had shrunk. He urged them to come closer, to his breast. Then he embraced them and uttered the words he'd repeated so often over the years, but in a different voice now. It was deep, growing ever slower, jerky, like the voice of a preacher sounding out from the folds of time: "Listen, now! If, some day, you become rich, then trade in gold. Don't buy land and lose everything you've won! My father and his grandfathers owned great tracts, thousands of acres. And where are they now? But for your mother's gold, we'd still be at the mosque where we took refuge when the migration started. Bodies were crammed there, in misery, with women wailing. What good did those thousands of acres do?"

He caught his breath and struggled to finish.

"But for your mother's gold! She had the wit to bring it with her. With that gold, by God, she kept you from hunger and beggary. She saved us from living in tents, spared us the shame of standing in tatters at the doors of the relief agency. My advice to you is—commerce. Commerce! Put the money in the bank and buy gold. Land? It's our nation's destiny to be abandoned by the land when we need it— foreigners are forever disputing it with us. I tell you. Always keep your money ready, to be there under your hand."

The deep voice had become firm and clear. It was Ihsan Natour's body that was unsteady; the room swimming in front of him. He'd thrust his fingers at the wall and found it dully solid.

Damn you, Faris! So he'd kept cursing as he traveled to Barqais for the first time, in a small two-engine plane; and his curses had redoubled when it landed on the water and he put his hand on its side, to find it was made of cloth and gave under the pressure! That flight to Barqais, he swore by all the prophets, took eight hours, with the plane leaning the whole way, this way and that.

At the start the stewardess had said it was a three-hour trip. When the plane started leaning to the right, he was gripped by a panic that moved from his temples right down to the soles of his feet.

Damn your father, *ustadh*![1] Ask me now to define the soles of my feet, and I'll know just how to answer you! I still remember my shame in front of my classmates. "Ihsan Natour," you yelled. "You stupid, lazy creature! Why haven't you memorized the definitions? Don't you know what the soles of your feet are, boy?"

Come with me in this plane, *ustadh*. Fly over deserts, and more deserts and sands, and learn your devilish lot. You won't need your books and definitions then, to know how fear can creep from the top of your head to the soles of your feet.

You can try memorizing it a thousand times, and it won't stay in your head. But when I felt the fear surging in my veins, I knew well enough. I knew from real life how to get where I wanted. Not by learning—all the sciences won't take me where I want to go. Life's the school. Did Faris get where he is through learning and schools?

Faris! Everyone used to stand up when he came into a place. They didn't think of him as a bad student; they pretended to forget he was illiterate. They set aside his squint too. It made him look distinguished, marked him out from other people! When Faris got money, people started enjoying his naive way of thinking, as he talked about things he didn't understand. But Faris's mind and fingers were magnets no money could get past. He was a natural merchant—he'd traded in everything, and commerce had won him respect and esteem.

It was money that let Faris marry your sister Afaf, even though your mother had never stopped cursing relatives, calling them scorpions. She didn't even give Afaf time to finish her studies. She married her off to him as soon as she'd finished preparatory school.

Commerce and business of all kinds got Faris what he wanted, even though he doesn't have a jot of your intelligence and education. Well, soon you'll be the successful one, and everyone, Faris included, is going to know who Ihsan Natour is!

What is it Faris never stops saying? "I started with a stall in Barqais, selling chickpeas and fava beans!" In summer, when he visits us in Damascus, his laugh booms out as he sees the attention he gets from everyone. He leans back, then he lifts his feet a fraction, above the soft Persian carpet he gave his mother-in-law as a present. His squint gets worse as he describes the crowds of employees and laborers, how they stand there for hours every saturday, waiting for the Dakota to arrive from Beirut.

"They're all the same, you take my word for it, when it comes to their bellies, or the Dakota! You can never fill people's bellies, they're bottomless. By God, there's the inspector, and the manager, and the laborer! They're all waiting for vegetables, fruit, crushed wheat, oil. They're all the same, you know that?"

He always, he swears, doles out the food according to the number in each family. Three lots for the manager, eight portions for that laborer. Everything right and proper!

Faris's drawers are stuffed with money and vast profits. Crowds waiting for the plane—crowds looking for chickpeas and fava beans—laborers—employees—families living in Barqais, their wives go out in public. By God, they're like hordes of refugees in front of the relief agency!

On he goes, laughing: "You know what, mother-in-law? The profit from one plane load is as much as the salaries of ten of those consultants with their plush offices, standing there in the line. You have to know where to make a profit, and how."

Well, Faris, I'll show you the sort of commerce you never dreamed of. The sort you can't even imagine.

Faris always laughed at people who were employed, big or small, who were happy with great offices and smart suits, who dealt with money by the millions but only ever saw it on paper. Meanwhile Faris's pockets, and the pockets of other sensible people, were bulging.

Faris started with a photographic studio, and he never stopped bragging about all his successes, whenever he came back from Barqais and people crowded around him to pay their respects or ask for a job there—or even, in some cases, ventured to ask for a loan or financial help.

Your mother, Ihsan, used to spend days preparing when he was due to come. She'd beat the Persian carpets Faris had given, polish the furniture, then burn incense and aloe-wood—he'd brought her that too, and taught her how to fill her house with fragrant smells the way people do in Barqais.

And Faris would repeat stories he'd told so many times before, and everyone would listen to them, expressing wonder and admiration, greedy for some of his gifts. You used to get fed up with him and his stories, Ihsan. That story about the Barqais cards—you'd heard it a hundred times.

The British governor had stipulated cards, permits, for anyone coming to work in Barqais—employees and laborers, along with their families. And Faris was ready. The moment he heard of this, from a simple Asian working as a printer in the Governor's office, he got hold of an Armenian photographer from Aleppo. He'd buy information by giving small gifts to minor employees, and they'd let him know what the big shots were thinking, before a directive was ever issued.

He thrust his hand under the black cloth, and took pictures until his drawers were overflowing with payments. Then he changed the machine for a photographic studio—a big, spacious place where people used to line up in front of that Armenian who spoke Arabic with such a funny, heavy accent. Lines of people talking different languages, adding to the discord. Lines of people seeking their fortune, standing there endlessly under the blazing sun.

Faris had realized, too, how foreigners tended to counter expatriation by reaching back to their torn-up roots, to where their relatives were and the people they knew, to their homelands—through photos and letters.

Faris alone saw how even banal, everyday things can grow dear, can seem beautiful and flawless; and how moments of longing stretch into threads that twine around you and engulf you, so that you yield to them, fly with them in a delightful torpor; and still the threads entwine, more and more—pressing on the neck and the head, then pouring down into the depths of the body, where they harden and clutch the breast with an urgent longing for what's far away.

Faris alone realized how a migrant counters expatriation with photographs. And so the lines in his shop grew, as people recorded their moments of longing and sent them to their people back home. Pictures of people in *dashdashas*[2]—in wrap-around garments—in other oriental garb—or else with their upper halves bare, their black faces made still blacker by the bad lighting. Smiling through eyes dazzled by the haze. Pictures beside thorny shrubs, on the calm sea shore, over hands roasting meat at low tide, in front of small, old wooden boats that still raced with their nets in search of a catch. By God, Faris! Photos and rupees, and still more rupees, until the big chance came along and he was ready for it. The printing press.

❧

Nadia was moving fitfully alongside him. She got up and dressed. Then she smiled, her head reclining against the top of the bed, her features starting to take on the appearance of wakefulness. Ihsan lost the desire to arouse her, gazing at her, instead, with a kind of wondering calm. He drew deeply on his cigarette, then blew out a cloud of smoke, which broke up and began drifting toward her.

"Nadia," he said, breaking the silence between them, "tomorrow I want all the women in Barqais to be talking about you."

"You don't know that bunch of women around the hostess," Nadia said. "They don't give anyone else a chance! Besides, I don't know most of the people who are going to be there. Look, I'm sorry, I just don't feel like going."

Ihsan became irritable.

"Nobody's asking you to make a speech, Nadia. The point is to let them see you, make them notice you."

She got restlessly back into bed and turned her back on him.

What goes on in that head of his? she thought. Can't he see he's tiring me out, thrusting me toward a great open sea? All these gatherings and parties. Women, and more women, and still more women, weighing one another up with smiles, and all the time, behind it, longing to spring and pounce on their prey. They flaunt their soft silks and their perfumes from Paris, but it can't hide the ugliness of those tongues, tearing into guests who've just left or the people who haven't come.

And all that cant and hypocrisy—wailing how they miss their beloved homelands far away. They chose to come and live abroad, didn't they? They certainly don't try and hide those glittering diamonds on their necks and wrists and fingers! Diamonds, and more diamonds, hiding backgrounds you can't be sure of half the time—as if it mattered anyway. They're all, apparently, the daughters of families with influence, descended from the cream of society. It makes you wonder if those far-off homelands ever had any farmers in them, or servants, or laborers, or small merchants maybe. Why does he keep trying to push me on to them?

"Nadia, I found this quite marvelous dress at Harrods. It cost the earth, from a top designer. You should have seen the salesgirls' eyes as they wrapped it up! Lucky wife, they were thinking, every one of them. Harrods! No one shops there except kings and princes and rich people."

She said nothing.

"If we really make it," he went on, "we'll go to London together this winter. I've never been there in winter. They say it's wonderful at Christmas time, with the snow on the ground."

Does he know where he's pushing me? Does he even care? Hasn't it ever struck him, just for a second, that I don't want all this—that I hate all these women's gatherings in Barqais? But no, he always knows best. Of course he does! Events have shown that, haven't they? And isn't he working for both our goods?

"That diamond set, Nadia. They'll all go wild with jealousy. It cost me nearly all I have. But you deserve more than just a set. Look, Nadia, if I really make it, I'll cover you in diamonds, right down to the soles of your feet."

He threw his head back and roared with laughter. She turned to him in surprise.

"What are you laughing at?"

He didn't answer. He kept seeing his old teacher's face as he scolded him.

"And why go to London in winter anyway? I can't stand the cold—in Damascus it used to chill me to the bone. I could feel the blood freezing in the tips of my fingers. They used to swell up. How am I going to stand the cold there?"

"I won't let you get cold, my kitten. Or make you get wet in the rain either!"

As he put his hand out to stroke her hair, she began muttering to herself, her heart sinking at the way he was talking. It made her feel ill when he called her his "kitten," but nothing would stop him from doing it. It hurt her, too, that he could never see her as anything but his woman. She didn't understand. Hadn't it occurred to him, just once, that she might have feelings beyond the ones he wanted from her?

He put his arm under her pillow, and she turned her head violently away. She smelled traces of her perfume on the edge of the pillow, and took satisfaction in his good taste.

~᪥᪥~

Ihsan was carrying the papers, and the blue file clutched to his chest, with the utmost care. He felt the file shaking, and fought to control his nerves. He sat down in the empty reception room.

Steady, Ihsan, he thought. Steady! Be sure to stay calm when he first sees you. Curse that first look! It can raise you to the heights, or else fling you down to the bottom of the mountain. The first look. Who said only love comes at first sight? It happens everywhere, and in business most of all. Why else are people's ends and destinies linked to one particular moment, not one second earlier or later? Special moments, plotted by some hidden force. Moments that don't just pass, and don't hold back either, decreed by the hand of fate to change your life!

Why do people keep saying hard work leads to success? Success comes from work maybe, but from luck too! And it's luck that really counts. If there were no luck involved, things would be easier for all those farmers who till the earth, and suffer, and die, water the soil with their sweat and misery and prayers. Each day they scratch at the soil with new hope—and still they wither and die poor. Why should a businessman, in one deal, reap what they have to suffer for decades to get? Then there's the gambler at the roulette wheel. With luck, mere luck, he wins what they, with all their struggle and toil, can't even imagine.

It's luck you need, Ihsan. And it'll come! A feeling deep

inside tells you it's coming. Wasn't that what the woman told you, when she begged you to let her read your fortune? That spring evening in Damascus, when you crept down a side street with her for fear someone might see you. She looked at your palm, then she threw her cowrie shells on a cloth spread over the pavement—and when she spoke all your misgivings melted away. She described the girl you were looking for in Nadia, and, to your delight, she assured you the girl would be yours and that your future stood wide ahead of you, because you were intelligent and blessed by your parents. You'd be great, you'd become a king. You gasped at that, and she added: "Not a real king. What I see, son, is authority and wealth."

You gave her everything you had in your pocket, then you walked back. This woman had affirmed what all the others never saw, that you'd surpass all the people you knew—and especially Jalal, the one they all admired so much! Jalal's only interested in making fine words, in studying and getting people's respect. But you're master and governor of yourself. Opinions and principles led Jalal down another road, while your convictions took you to Barqais. There's Jalal talking, pontificating, and the agencies and media talk about him along with all the others. They're even getting to hear of him in Barqais now, whereas you've been here for years and still can't get where you want to be. So, is that moment of luck coming today?

Jalal finished his studies. You did two years, then lost patience. You chose to join Faris in Barqais, find a short cut.

The fragrance of incense preceded His Highness, may he live long,[3] as he entered the reception room, and the sound his footwear made was in harmony with the rustle of his cloak and gown. Ihsan stood up. His Highness stepped closer, but Ihsan advanced to meet him, then greeted him. They shook hands. The man had an impressive air, and, seen close up, was older than Ihsan had thought; up to now he'd only glimpsed him riding in his black Mercedes. Threads of white were visible among the strands of the black beard, and Ihsan realized at once that it was dyed. Threads of time, too, were clustered around the pupils of his eyes, giving him the look of a hawk swooping and pouncing, the blindfold just taken from its eyes, blurring the sight for a few moments.

He gazed intently into Ihsan's face, then his friendly look returned. Still holding on to Ihsan's hand, he walked him to the front of the big room, which, with its clusters of chairs and rugs, looked less ugly, an air of affable friendliness pervading them.

"Welcome," he said. "So, you're from the Natour family. What relation are you to Jalal Natour?"

Ihsan controlled his anger. Don't expect, he told himself, to get what you want straight off. He'd known in advance he'd be asked about Jalal, though he hadn't supposed the question would start the conversation off. Taking a grip of himself, he set out to exploit the opening as best he could.

"You know, Your Highness, it doesn't matter these days whether or not someone's the son of a well-known family. A person becomes important through his work. Even the sons of families of standing sometimes have to take any job they can to earn their bread—especially the sons of our nation—"

The man broke in abruptly, though there was sympathy and understanding in his voice.

"But Jalal Natour—isn't he your brother?"

"Yes, my blood brother."

"We follow what they're doing all the time—their latest operations. Your brother's a marvelous man, and we're with them completely in many matters. We're bound to be. They should make the world aware of their cause."

He leaned back and, from the side of his armchair, held up a cane Ihsan hadn't noticed earlier. A cane cut from a big *nabk* tree, then polished for his use, with a simple, old-fashioned air. He began tapping the rug with the end of it, and moving it around as though drawing something. Then, abruptly, he left his thoughts.

"And you, Ihsan," he said. "Are you one of them?"

"Your Highness," Ihsan replied, "we're two brothers, along with two sisters, one of them widowed and living with my mother. If both of us were to leave, things would be very difficult for them and my mother—"

Suppose His Highness were ever to discover that the brother-in-law, when he died, had left his sister a small fortune? And that he, Ihsan, had refused to join with Jalal because he was bent on a different course? No, he assured himself, the man wouldn't find out.

A look of sympathy appeared on the wise face opposite him, and the eyes had an admiring glint.

"God bless you and grant you success. But tell me, Ihsan, how do Jalal and his comrades get—"

The white-clad servant sprang up soundlessly in front of them. He'd advanced barefoot, with the coffee pot in his right hand and some cups in the other. Ihsan was startled, and the final word hovered over His Highness's lips. Oh, God in heaven! Surely he'd been about to utter the magic word! Out it would have come, without further ado, heralding a talk that would have been short, quiet, flowing like a smooth stream, the ease of it transcending all his strategies and plans. Everything had been forthcoming— making the heart leap, the nerves quiver in anticipation—

and then in had come this barefoot beggar to spoil Ihsan's moment. Damn him, and his coffee too!

The servant poured a little in the first cup, and the air was redolent with cardamom, saffron, and coffee. Bowing respectfully to His Highness, the man held out the cup. He straightened, then passed the second cup to Ihsan, who felt its heat as the servant studied him curiously.

Ihsan was now used to the special taste of Barqais coffee, which was yellowish, light, and left no grounds. He drank it constantly at Faris's place, and at the office of Abdulrahman al-Hemli where he worked. It was so different from his mother's coffee, brewed black in a *rakwa*.[4] After he'd drunk it, she'd always insist on upturning the cup and trying, vainly, to read the magic in the grounds.

Eight years earlier, just two days before he left, his mother had sat gazing at her neighbor, who'd made him drink his cup of coffee on an empty stomach, while Jalal's face registered ironic doubt. His luck was amazing, the woman declared, the future wide and vast before him.

That devil was still standing there in front of them, waiting for something. Ihsan remembered and shook the cup several times—upon which the servant went off with his things as soundlessly as he'd come in. His Highness smiled once more.

Moments of waiting are whole ages that grow ever longer as the phantoms of anxiety, and fear, and apprehension, silently flit. The huge room was plunged deep in silence now, as each waited for the other to speak.

The expression on the generous, confident face was utterly friendly, quite open. Why had he been so afraid of meeting this man, spent so long calculating and planning the hunt? Now this face had torn down all the walls he'd striven, in his imagination, to build up between them. He'd started building and destroying ever since the owner of the company, Abdulrahman al-Hemli, had informed him of the date of the meeting—and, now he'd met the man, all his plans had come tumbling down before this open face, with its spontaneity and friendly warmth.

It was His Highness who began.

"Now then, Ihsan," he said, suddenly but quite straightforwardly. "Jalal and his comrades. How do they get their arms?"

Ihsan's heart leaped, piercing his ribs almost. He'd planned for so long to pry this question out of the man. How could he ask it so simply?

"Your Highness, arms aren't their problem—it's money."

"Ah, yes, money. You can get arms from all sorts of places. It's money that's the issue."

He made a jerky movement of his cane toward Ihsan.

"God send you light, Ihsan!" he said, his tone sarcastic now. "Money? What about the aid we send them? Millions, man! Why are you talking about money?"

"Jalal's group gets only part of it. That's one of the reasons, as you know, for disputes between them and the others."

His Highness's smile was half dubious, half ironic.

"How is it they have no problem getting hold of arms? Even countries have problems, man! God send you light, how can that be?"

"It's never any problem for them. They have plenty of avenues open. It's money they find difficult."

The man propped his cane against the side of the chair and started cracking his fingers one after the other. Then he leaned forward, reflecting for a time, while Ihsan remained watchful, ready to grasp the opportunity.

"And you, Ihsan," His Highness said suddenly, in a tone of great interest. "Are you happy with al-Hemli? Are your affairs prospering, God willing?"

He was no fool, this man! Ihsan made an effort to follow his drift. Why had he suddenly changed the subject, apparently losing interest? How was it he'd broached the matter, then suddenly dropped it?

"Abdulrahman's a good man," he replied. "He has complete faith in me, and in the finance manager. That, thank God, makes business easier and gives us scope to expand."

His Highness relaxed his fingers, leaned back, then took his cane once more and began moving it over the carpet.

Should you have said something else to please him, Ihsan? he thought. But you can't run down al-Hemli or try and harm him, after all those wide horizons he's opened for you. Abdulrahman's ambitions are the same as yours, to make plenty of money, and enjoy it. Besides, this man in front of you is deeper and cleverer than you thought. Still, Ishan kept his nerve for all his uncertainty and confusion.

"Well, that's fine, Ihsan! And the project that brings you here, what is it?"

Ihsan spread the papers from the blue file over the small table, in front of his host. Finding the table a little too far away, he tried to pull it closer, but couldn't move the heavy marble. His Highness watched him briefly, then said: "Leave the papers, Ihsan. Just tell me what it is you want."

"Your Highness, the whole region's expanding, and so is Barqais, with its growing oil production—in a few months the canal will be fully open—companies around the world are interested in running giant carriers. We've had an offer from an American company, A Octane International, one of the oldest established companies in America, to build a new dock in Barqais capable of taking these huge carriers."

His Highness pursed his lips, bit the lower one, then fixed his eyes on Ihsan's.

"But," Ihsan went on, "there's something more important than the dock——"

His Highness raised his teeth from his lips, which had a reddened look now. Ihsan's senses were on the alert.

You shouldn't have said that, Ibn Natour,[5] he thought. How are you going to get out of it now? You fool! How can you talk about this or that aim being more important, when all your aims are equal in your dreams? You can't back out now, though. You ought to be more careful.

"What's more important," he went on, "is to build a special system in the sea of Barqais, for maintenance and repair of the carriers, and for the drilling ships belonging to all the oil companies working in Barqais."

His Highness sat there calmly, turning things over in his mind. Ihsan, having said all he had to say, was silent too.

"It's an interesting project," His Highness said. "But what are the Americans asking?"

"What they're asking is very reasonable—not much at all. A Octane would undertake the enlargement of the dock for the Barqais government at a very low price, and it could be tendered internationally as the government wished. As for ship repairs, they would be free—a gift from the company."

The other man's smile was ironic and scathing. He'd seen what the game was faster than Ihsan would have thought possible.

"Free! Ha, ha! Those American pimps never do anything for free!"

"Well, there is a condition. They're proposing a ten-year contract for repairing the ships and equipment in all the

Barqais oil fields. After that the system would become the property of the government, but the divers and engineers of A Octane would stay for a further five years to supervise operations."

His Highness was silent for a long time. He tugged his cane toward him and started once more moving it over the rug. That, Ihsan recalled later, was what the man did whenever he was preoccupied with a serious matter. As the silence stretched on, the walls seemed to acquire a dark and gloomy depth, the surrounding colors to grow discordant and ugly.

Would the man's native intelligence tell him how most of the international companies had started opening branches in Houston? That they were battling and spying on each other, all seeking tricky ways to gain access for their giant ships?

Would he be persuaded to give A Octane monopoly of this business and make all Ihsan's dreams come true? If he only would, then the matter could go to the Shyoukh,[6] who had the final say. The Shyoukh was actually just one man, but he was everything in one, and referred to, with profound respect, in the plural form. His Highness, it was true, was head of a clan and had, as a minister, been very close to the Shyoukh since the days before independence, when Barqais was still under British control. It was also true he was entrusted with all the business in Barqais, parceling it out among everyone while keeping a lot of it for himself. Would he be persuaded by what Ihsan had said?

"Ihsan," he said suddenly, "do you know Rashid?"

Why did he have to cut through the crucial moment, draining it of decisive quality, with an irrelevant question like that? That, though, was his way, the manner in which he worked. You had to know how to deal with him, and be well prepared with plans and designs of your own.

"We've met casually," he said. "On a few social occasions."

"Rashid's a splendid young man. He comes from one of the most important families in Lebanon."

"The company, Your Highness, would like to keep the matter just between the two of you until the final decision's reached. After that, Rashid and the others could be informed. The company's aware of your high standing with the Shyoukh, and attaches great importance to your understanding of its project. It might be possible, in case of agreement, to expand the dock in conjunction with your contracting company, at the rate you decided. Once the system was built, though, the company would sign an agreement to equip the site with a catering business. Rashid would know about all this once the agreement was signed. In the meantime, the company would greatly appreciate it if you could see your way to keeping the matter confidential."

"Rashid's loyal. You can trust him to be discreet."

Why this persistence in thrusting Rashid into the business? That young fellow from Tripoli! He'd met him once or twice at parties, a most elegant bachelor in a full silk shirt, smiling in a distinctly self-satisfied way. He'd had people all around him as he emphasized his influence and how much His Highness admired him.

"A secret between more than two, Your Highness, isn't a secret any more. Didn't our Prophet say: 'Seek discretion to achieve your goals?' Discretion means not telling even those closest to you."

His Highness laughed, apparently convinced.

"Very well, Ihsan. Just give me a few days to look the matter over, then I'll give you my answer. Pass by my room a week from now, and we'll see."

The servant returned suddenly, carrying a censer. Standing at some distance from His Highness, he placed the aloe wood over a live coal, then passed it to his master, who moved the aromatic wood in front of his face, so that the fragrance permeated his clothes and the hairs of his beard. After some moments he gave it back to the servant, who extended it to Ihsan. For some moments the censer passed between them in silence; and when the servant finally took it out, a hazy cloud remained above their heads, raining down fragrance.

Ihsan remembered a saying Abdulrahman always repeated. "No more sitting after the incense." He asked permission to leave, and his host got up. Ihsan gathered his papers and rose himself. Then his fingers reached unconsciously for the buttons of his jacket, which he did up respectfully.

His Highness beamed and shook him by the hand.

TWO

Of the Arabian's Lineage

These streets beneath his speeding car dozed in the noonday heat, leaping as the yellow sands blazed. Along their sides stood a few straggly, thorny shrubs, clinging to life despite the flaming September haze that burned their tips. There were houses here and there, some close together, others scattered, the old mingling with lofty new ones standing aloof within their walls.

The people of Barqais, he thought, are natural merchants. They build houses for newcomers, so as to suck in with their left hand what they grant with their right. The flaming heat consumes us both, and we squander great sums to combat it. Air conditioners roaring away night and day—in houses, cars, offices, everywhere.

He was struck by a cold blast from the one in his Mercedes, and he turned it down. Oh, that first car, he thought, how did I stand it? I had to be patient, there was no air conditioning. You know how it breaks down at noon. Curse the father of poverty—poverty and heat! It's fearful. In a car without air conditioning, in the Barqais summer, you come to know how heat can flow into your limbs, numbing and paralyzing you. How it can storm your very mind and sap your energy. They talk of the north and the south. If the heat of the southern deserts ever invaded the north, where it's so blessedly cool the whole time, their minds and bodies wouldn't function any more. But it's in the wretched south that the heat strikes, putting every sort of ability to sleep. That's why the north's the prosperous place, the creative one, while the south stays poor and indebted.

There's a divine wisdom in all this, Ihsan, he thought. A divine wisdom whose essence we don't comprehend. We know nothing of what lies behind it.

A year after he'd arrived in Barqais, when he'd saved enough for a first installment, he'd bought the Mercedes. That had made Faris yell—Faris had given him a lecture. But Faris, he thought, is a mule. He doesn't understand what goes on in your mind, and he never will.

Those who'd come with Faris had made their fortunes easily enough. Barqais had been a place of scattered houses then, and it needed everything. The people were simple and primitive, which made it easy to succeed.

It had grown today, expanded. It still lacked many things, it was true, but there were plenty of opportunists and success didn't come easy any more. But you, Ihsan, he thought, you won't start small the way Faris did, you won't accept anything less than the summit. That's where your wars and victories are going to happen.

How far off that day seemed now, when the mountains of Damascus had stood so loftily, daring him that spring afternoon. They'd never seemed so alive as at that moment. The greenery was everywhere, and his mother, there among the other women, was calling to him. Shouting. But on he galloped, toward the peak. When she couldn't catch up with him, she repeated that inexplicable saying of hers:

"How I fear for you from yourself, son."

The other boys, seeing him climbing, galloped after him, their cries rising higher as he ran on ahead of them, toward the summit. The thorns, and the rock and pits, were hidden by all the leaves. As he surged on, Jalal came up close behind, for he was racing upward too and Ihsan was beginning to feel the spring wind against him.

He tripped over a stone and tumbled painfully, the blood spurting from a gash in his knee. In his pain, he pulled as hard as he could at Jalal's clothes, and Jalal fell over him as he tried to overtake him. Jalal hadn't noticed his bleeding wound. He simply cursed his brother, the way children do, freed himself and raced on ahead. Ihsan crumpled, sat there on the ground and wept, not from pain but out of bitter anguish that Jalal had overtaken him. He kept on shouting, through his tears: "Aah! My knee!"

Jalal stopped and turned around, then, spotting the wounded knee, ran back to him. For a moment he stood there confused; then he hugged Ihsan, his eyes holding a fear and affection that were love. As the first racer approached, a boy in short pants, he gave no sign of his pain. How did he endure that pain? He was smiling to himself now.

He thrust his hand in the earth, which was still moist from recent rain and warm from the spring sun. The sun over the summit isn't going to burn you, he thought. He called the boy in the short pants by name. The boy turned, surprise in his eyes, and Ihsan smudged his young features with mud. Another handful thrown into Jalal's questioning eyes, and there he was, their attention distracted, racing on, enduring his hurt, hopping on one leg! On he ran, the air striking his face, making his bleeding wound sting.

The summit became his alone, the earth, and spring, and the women and children all beneath him.

Jalal's racing to a summit of his own, he thought. It's a different peak, but a summit's still a summit. The first to reach it sits on top, no matter what the difference in the tracks and paths.

Here in Barqais nature was yellow; it was laid out and exposed, without slope or height, not standing high to dare you. There the lofty mountains were wrapped in wonderment. How they stretched out! What were they hiding beyond themselves? The seasons changed, and the mountains still drew you on, whether bare with winter, or dressed in the greenery of spring, or aged by the heaping snow. Their trees soared up, so different from these thorny shrubs vying with the dunes that rose shyly around them.

But it was the sands, he thought, that had flung up the black blessing. By a sacred wisdom, Ihsan, those summits stayed poor for all their beauty, no fortunes were ever conceived within them. By a sacred wisdom those fortunes were buried in the bowels of the sands. So, make your summit over them. Conquer them and let Nadia be by your side.

Tenderness surged through him as he remembered her. He smiled, telling himself of his love for her, even if she didn't share his ambition.

At any rate, he reflected, she obeys you absolutely. She even stopped reading books for your sake. She'd shout once, and get angry, if ever you took away her book. But you managed to distract her, make her forget, and she gave in to you. Nadia hardly ever reads now. She's done that because she loves you. And you love her—you wanted her from the start! Just as Jalal loved her and wanted her. Does he still think of her? And did Nadia ever realize just what happened?

No, there was no way she could have known.

At sunset you intercepted him as the two of you came down the mountain. Two young men, Jalal in his third year of studies, you still struggling with your first. You approached him. He was raising his collar, trying to ward off the night cold and whistling a beautiful tune. You went hurrying down the slope together. You'd seized the moment, but you'd planned it too. As Jalal kept walking, you said, your voice controlled and affectionate: "Jalal, your brother's really struck, plunged in deep to the knees. I'm in love, Jalal."

Jalal stopped whistling, but went on climbing down. Then the words came out through his collar, indifferent. "You? You'll never know how to love."

It wasn't the answer itself that bothered you. Just his indifference. You wanted him to turn and face you, to see his anxiety, the wonderment in his eyes and voice. You wanted him to beg you to reveal her name, so you could blast your missile in his face! He went back to his careless whistling—and you controlled your anger, so as to cherish the moment.

"Jalal? Do you know Nadia?"

He stopped now. Turned around, let his collar go, so that his hair fluttered. His pupils widened, made handsome by his astonishment.

"You mean Nadia al-Faqih?"

Ecstasy whirled through your limbs. He hadn't missed the point, hadn't wondered. He'd known who she was the moment you spoke her name. You were certain he felt the same way about her as you did. That he'd followed her with his eyes since she'd started growing up. Did he really want her? Was she filling his imagination too? No, don't ask him, Ihsan.

The question would show your cards, spoil your plans. The thing to do is to attack Jalal and take her away from him, as if you'd never even noticed his interest. That's the way to win your battle.

"Yes, that's right. Nadia al-Faqih."

Was he still thinking about her now? No. Out of the question. Not Jalal, however fond he'd been of her. When he was a boy, and you competed with him to get something, he'd put up some small resistance, but he always ended up giving you what you wanted—happy enough with praise and his parents' approval. And you'd get what you wanted. Even when your mother would lose hope as you stumbled on, declaring you'd never get anywhere, he'd take your side and reassure her, playing the part of eldest son in an eastern family—the eldest brother, who's supposed to be unselfish and make sacrifices. His brothers and sisters make him their slave, ride on his back, but he's content to believe that's how things have to be with the first-born. Jalal hadn't seriously thought to be like Esau, the Jew whose story he'd read somewhere in the Old Testament, who'd sold his birthright for a dish of lentils. Before telling you the story, he'd said to you jokingly: "Ihsan, would you like to buy my birthright for a pot of lentils, so I can get you off my back? You've always hated lentils anyway, ever since you were a child and your mother sweated to prepare them. It didn't matter what pickles or green leaves she put in with them, or if she mixed the things with rice or dough. You only hated them all the more. They were horrible things, you thought, demeaning your table two or three times a week. Then, when your father got that post in Damascus, there were fewer lentil meals and you wouldn't eat the things any more.

And then—there you sat, reading a French menu in that little restaurant by the Seine, your finger stuck under a word you couldn't pronounce—and the waiter smiled and nodded his head. It was lentil soup, following you all the way to Paris!"

༄

Faris never stops telling, at every gathering, how the people who came first would die of the fearful heat, lying there like dead meat under the blazing sun.

That recalls the story of the bride Faris so endlessly repeats. The wife of one of his staff had become pregnant straight after her marriage, her swollen belly making her look still more beautiful. White and delicate, Ihsan thought, that's how I see her. I've heard the story so many times I feel I know her now. Wide eyes, just nineteen years old, daughter of a refugee camp. There was only one air conditioner in her home, which became almost useless when the heat peaked. Unable to stand it any longer, she poured water on the floor—and kept on pouring.

The question always nagged me. What made her even think of doing it? What spurred her on to iron her husband's clothes in that heat? Was it to kill time? Or had she been afraid her labor would come on suddenly and she wouldn't be able to see to his needs any longer? How silly! Was she maybe descended from that Arabian woman who endlessly advised her children to serve the husband and see to his comfort?

No one knew quite what happened. Her blackened body was found lying on the damp floor, the wires of the iron exposed and still working when her husband got back. With time her face grew lovelier still in my imagination.

I often thought of that woman. Her image stayed with me. Still she glowed in my memory, and grew more slender, until at last she was as graceful as a doe, with a flat belly—delicate as a rose—elegant and aspiring. But she'd died tragically. According to Faris, she'd been beautiful but utterly simple too, come from a small village in that distant homeland to join her prize bridegroom, who worked in Barqais, enjoyed the wealth of an oil country. She'd stood there in the heat, ironing his things so as to please him. Where's all that heat now, with the cooling breeze of air conditioners everywhere?

⌐✿¬

Nadia didn't raise her eyes from her book as Ihsan came laughing into the room. She just went on reading. How beautiful she still was, Ihsan thought, even though her waist had thickened now and no longer matched the shoulders onto which the hair fell black and shining, emphasizing their broadness. She refused to give up those tight skirts, ignoring Ihsan when he told her how they showed up the faults in her figure. She'd meet it all with silence, then go on wearing them.

Now, though, he resisted the urge to criticize, as she raised her child-like face toward him and he saw that radiance once more—saw the face he loved as if bewitched by a spell. He always regarded her looks as a good omen. She folded the corner of the page she was reading and set the book down beside her. He picked it up and leafed through it, noting the small print and long chapters, then tossed it aside.

"You'll hurt your eyes," he said.

How, he wondered, could she show such patience? She and Jalal? Jalal was forever reading. Crazy the pair of them, by God! They wasted their time on the pages of books when life, after all, was the best school and culture. What was the point of it? There was Jalal, he thought, endlessly memorizing books, endlessly discussing things, theorizing about things. But you, Ihsan, you're the clever one: you just read what's written on the back cover, then dip in here and there—and in the end you know pretty much the same as he does. And you don't just profit from the bits you read, you learn from his comments too.

"Where are the magazines then, Nadia?" he asked. "What artists have divorced or married this week?"

The joke had grown stale now. She looked away, saying nothing, then leaned back in her chair. Why, she thought, must he always belittle everything? This book in my hand irritates him. From the first day of our marriage he'd make a point of pulling it from my hands, until at last I'd set it aside when he came into the room. I wanted to be his wife! I spring, don't I, from that bedouin woman long ago, whose advice to her daughters has been passed down through generations of women? "Do whatever he tells you. Keep all his secrets. Let him find only the purest fragrance in you." I wanted to be that skillful woman who wraps her husband around with love and tenderness. He took that good book from my hands, and put stupid magazines in their place, and I read them! He asked me what was in them, and I told him. When we came to Barqais, he planted me among the families of his friends, among people who thought of nothing but money and getting money. The emptiness started hemming me in. I felt it when I was with him, and when I was with other people, until I began to feel stifled.

"Nadia," Ihsan said, "you haven't asked me what's happened today. My plans are working out, and quicker than you think too."

He rubbed his hands happily. She said nothing.

"What do you say," Ihsan went on, "to visiting his wife and daughters? You need to get on good terms with them. The man's the height of good taste and kindness. All my dreams are bound up with him."

To his surprise she sat up in irritation.

"For heaven's sake, Ihsan," she said impatiently, "do whatever you want. Plan and scheme to your heart's content. Just don't involve me in your games. I can't take any more of this."

"Of course you can! You're beautiful and intelligent. You really must get rid of this silly shyness."

He raised her face toward him. It wore the expression that had puzzled him for so long now—that same mixture of surrender and rejection. And now, for the first time, the rejection had been expressed in words.

"You've had three children," Ihsan went on, "and you're still as shy as a new bride! You'll have to change, my lovely kitten, because our life's going to change, believe me."

She jerked his hand from her chin.

"For heaven's sake, Ihsan," she said, "will you please stop calling me by that wretched name! Do whatever you like. Just don't get me mixed up in your schemes."

Does he ever think, she wondered, of what happens to me now? Has he any idea, when he sees me as his "woman," of the way a great snake bites at me? A rebellious snake, but helpless too. It coils around, deep inside me. There's another person there inside me, sexless, a person who feels and thinks and suffers, and makes me suffer.

A person who doesn't know the meaning of female and male, who rises above anything Ihsan ever thinks about. It burns me with its whip whenever Ihsan enjoys arousing the female in me. But it's a suffering too, weak and suppressed, powerless to rise to resistance and refusal, when Ihsan treats me as his toy, then goes happily off to sleep. I lean on the edge of the bed, overwhelmed by a sense that's inscrutable, akin to a vision. And there, at the edge of the bed, a pit opens, yawning and bottomless. I'm cloaked in a light dizziness, and I slip, then I plunge, helpless, into the thick darkness—toward the pit, not knowing how far it goes down, how far it stretches, and I've no power to stop.

I tremble, then take hold of myself. How many times has this happened? So many! Is it a vision? Or is it a feeling, or a fantasy? It's been with me a long time now. It grew stronger after my third child was born.

We surrender again, my defeated person and I, when next Ihsan approaches and enfolds me, looking for the woman in me. Winter wraps my rebellion around, blocks my vision. I long for a season of spring, from which my inner self bursts out, revealing the human being I want to be and possess, one who rebels and mutinies and rejects. I know now, since we've been married, how he's been rushing around, matching his strength with competitors and phantoms, the phantom of Faris the strongest of all. When Faris came to Barqais, the city became a different world.

How often I've wished Ihsan was like Jalal! If I'd married Jalal, surely he would have understood me better. Jalal's cultured, different altogether. He would have sensed what I was going through; I wouldn't have needed to explain. He wanted me—there was no mistaking his looks as he followed me. He did that so many times, through the alleys of Damascus—then stopped as suddenly as he'd started. He wouldn't even look at me. I used to try, deliberately, to let him see me, but he'd lower his eyes, then vanish. If he'd loved me, would he have let his younger brother marry me? "You're full of fancies," they used to tell me. "You build castles in the air." A romantic, building a castle from a single tender word. Perhaps I am. His face did change, even so, each time he saw me, revealing something he couldn't hide. Ihsan used to fondle and hug me more when Jalal was there, and in a different way too. Or am I just imagining things?

"So, what do you say, Nadia? Will you go?"

"Please! Just leave me out of it. Be successful, the way you want to be. You can do that without me. I've tried already, and I can't stand that whole atmosphere. Do you know how things are there? Every one of those women wears a set of different masks, changing from one to another the moment you turn away from her. Their minds are split—they're driven blind by boredom. Several times now I've been there, for your sake, and I'm not going any more. Do you know what it means, to have to be someone you're not? What's the point of it? Do what you want and let me be."

"The things in those books have taken you over," Ihsan said. "All these impetuous, cultured people and their rebellious ways! You must stand by me. You must stand by me, just this once. Then I won't ask you again."

"I'm not going, Ihsan."

"Of course you are. You're a sensible woman, aren't you, who stands by her husband and supports him?"

He ruffled my hair, then went off to his room.

The person inside me moved. I felt it wake as Ihsan thrust me toward the slope. I hate to be what I'm not, to smile when I'm not happy, to repeat words I don't believe, to kill time in empty reception room talk, where there's only hypocrisy and falsehood. I waited to hear the person inside me scream, refuse to go, stand firm in the face of Ihsan. But then I felt it go limp, as Ihsan vanished behind his door. I cried out, silently, for it to come to my aid, to speak of the nausea that rises because everything's false and unreal around me.

Tell Ihsan how much we've suffered, you and I. I remember when you first started beating on the walls of my soul, the day that activist, Najwa Thabit, stood up at the head of the table. If you could talk of a table, that is—it stretched on and on! There were seven grilled lambs shining with fat, set on beds of rice fragrant with saffron, with countless broiled chickens arranged around them, decked with parsley and covered in boiled eggs and raisins and pine seeds and nuts, and all the other dishes there, filled with food of every kind and color. There's enough here, I thought, to feed a whole refugee camp. The idea shocked me. Did Najwa Thabit think as I did? She didn't so much as stretch out her hand, didn't try anything.

When the hostess called her to the table, the smell of food mingled with the smells of incense and women's perfume. The air conditioners were roaring on all sides. The servant brought in a box covered in blue velvet, which the hostess took, then handed to Najwa Thabit.

"This," she said, "is my father's sword, handed down by his own father. When my mother died, he gave it to me. There's nothing more precious than your revolution, to offer this sword to."

Najwa Thabit opened the box, and the gold blazed out, the diamonds and rubies glittered in the brilliance from the great chandeliers on the ceiling. Najwa Thabit's face stayed calm, though her eyes shone with dazzled wonderment. After a few moments she took hold of herself. Had she ever seen anything remotely like it?

A doctor's wife began to ululate, then cried out: "A generous woman, the daughter of a generous man! May God bless the womb that bore you! All your life you've been with us!"

Then everyone present burst into applause, to the hostess's exuberant joy. She stood there proudly with her short frame, her plump figure showing clearly through the long robe. Najwa Thabit had no choice but to respond.

Was it her slow, deliberate manner that didn't fit? Didn't fit the anxious look in the hostess's eyes, or the expectant air of the women who'd lifted their full plates once more, or the curiosity of those gazing at the glitter of the sword and the vast size of the diamonds and rubies set in its hilt? Najwa Thabit closed the blue velvet box and set it down by the side of the table. Then, moving her eyes over the people's faces, she launched, unexpectedly, into a forceful speech.

"In the name of the revolution," she said, "I should like to thank Her Highness, and her people here, for having always been with us. Here in Barqais you eat lambs, while our people live in camps that are often demolished over their heads. They suffer poverty and want. If each of you would stop for a moment, reflect on the people's plight there, many families could live and scores of young people have an education. We need support, financial support. And those who strive with their money are equal to those who strive with their lives. All we need is for you to pay for amenities."

"There's no strife," Her Highness broke in, "like the strife of the spirit."

"To hell with her," one of the other women muttered. "How about the five percent they take off our salaries each month? What do these people think we are? Do they think we own a bank?"

"She won't be happy," another whispered, "until she's taken all our salaries. So the revolution can buy Persian carpets!"

Did Najwa Thabit hear the whispers? She ended her speech abruptly, and the women sighed with relief. The place was filled with the sounds of knives and forks and the chink of plates.

And I, Nadia al-Faqih, felt the person inside me rebelling, kicking, revolting against all this falsehood. Here our homeland was a song, a dress, a hanger. It had vanished as reality. When I came here first, I thought the homeland was planted deep in people's hearts. So often I'd heard them sing about it. But where was it when our help was needed?

Like her I didn't touch the food. For all those roaring air conditioners, I started to feel the sweat trickle down my body, felt the heat about to stifle me, until I was ready to die from distress.

Ihsan was there, holding on to the door.

"We're agreed then, are we, Nadia?" he said. "You'll go."

"All right. But this is the last time!"

"My darling!" he cried joyfully.

He blew a kiss toward me, then vanished behind the door with a grin both happy and ironic.

Each time I threaten this will be the last. And each time he knows I can't refuse him. I used to stand out against attending these gatherings of women, all devoured by boredom, with nothing to talk about but money, and clothes, and perfumes, and husbands. Men have their world, and women too have their own, restricted world. There they'll sit, waiting for their husbands to return from their work or pleasures. Then in comes the man, heavy with fatigue, his waiting wife eaten up with longing. He's a man who vents an urge, while she's a woman looking for talk and tender affection, which she finds only with women like herself. The years pass, and he's still a man and she's still a woman.

I'm no different from the others. I left everything I loved when the man came for me, and I became his wife. Marriage filled my mind, pushing me to the tunnels of the unknown, gripped by wonder. I was consumed with desire to discover, to learn all about that secret unknown. It was a dark maze hemmed in with danger, a dim happiness I couldn't conceive; something we weren't allowed to discover. We'd etched its image on our minds, from what we'd heard, as small girls, whispered by women in our mothers' reception rooms. A comment or a gesture would escape from one of them; and then winks would be exchanged, and even the most straightlaced would laugh. And we'd hover around them, desperate to know. But all we'd get was a scolding, and one of them would laugh gaily and cry out:

"Shame on you! There are girls here!"

The tunnels are still surrounded by danger and dread, and the question that finds no answer: "So why do mothers go on accepting the danger?"

Only once we're flung into these tunnels can we come to know the experience the law allows. Marriage was the aim—a strange, confused feeling, somewhere between getting a husband and finding love.

Have I just grown used to Ihsan there in my life, or do I love him? I couldn't afford to wait for Jalal. Just as I began thinking of him at night, in my fantasy, he started to withdraw, vanishing whenever he saw me. I was a girl looking for marriage and love together, and Ihsan was ready to give me both. And so I agreed.

Ihsan would keep popping up in front of me, on this sidewalk and that—everywhere, all the time—it stirred a sense of satisfaction in me, how he kept following me—but if my eyes started following Jalal, Jalal would vanish the instant he caught sight of me.

I was waiting for the results of my baccalaureate exams, and brooding about Jalal, when I heard Ihsan call my name. I stopped abruptly on the sidewalk. The summer dusk was beautiful, like something in a poem—I was still trembling as he came up to me. He actually grasped my hand, leaving me confused, and asked to meet me next day. He had something important to tell me. I lay awake that night, torn between the two of them. Then, at the time arranged, I hurried to meet Ihsan, and everything was fixed between us, before he left to work in Barqais.

In the ten years since we were married, I've done what he wanted. He insisted I become pregnant, got to know the signs of my monthly period—waiting all the time—and when my body wouldn't respond to nature, he'd rant and rave because I couldn't conceive. Months went by. He'd start having doubts, urge me on. I wished then I could plant his fetus in my womb with my own hands. A fearful thought took me over. Might it be I was different, that I couldn't conceive? I stopped my studies that year, even though Ihsan and my mother had agreed I should finish them after we were married. I was preparing for second year finals. But I couldn't think of anything beyond proving I could be a mother. After months of ceaseless worry the doctor confirmed I was pregnant, and we both relaxed.

I'd proved my womanhood, and back I went to my

books, to make up for the year lost. But Ihsan wouldn't let me plunge into reading. He was so affectionate, so concerned, devising things to distract me. Then, a few months before the exams, he demanded a second pregnancy, and another year was lost.

Why did I let him plan the first chapter of my life? Let him shroud the hazy marriage in great, broad dreams and bury them there, while I stood silently watching?

᠂᠇᠊᠊᠆

When Ihsan got back to Nadia, he found her lost in thought. He poured himself a drink, sat down beside her and embraced her tenderly. Gently and calmly she removed his arm and laid it down on his legs.

"Do you know this story, Ihsan?" she asked. "Have you read it? It's about some men who were roasted to death in a tank because they didn't dare rap on the sides to be let out. They were being smuggled across the desert in the searing heat, but their terror was stronger than the urge for life itself. And so they died."[7]

He took a sip from his glass.

"Why are you bringing that up, Nadia?" he asked, managing to hide his astonishment. "The writer had lived in the desert, didn't you know? He must have heard the story and written it down. Faris knows some more terrible stories still. The people who came here first went through a lot."

Did he understand what I meant? Why do I never manage to say what I mean? Why do I expect him to understand the things I don't say?

He reflected for a moment, then his face relaxed.

"Education doesn't come from books, Nadia," he went on.

"Life teaches more. Look at Jalal. My father, God rest his soul, used to call him the library mouse. He'd spend his pocket money on second-hand books, from a small shop near the gate to the university. He didn't have much to spend, and so of course he learned to pick out the ones with a high-flown style. His trick was to stuff his brains with them, then pour them out on other people."

He treated himself to another sip, then went on to elaborate.

"Some people don't know how to grab a chance when it comes along. Especially the ones who like to call themselves cultured. Just think, Nadia, Jalal and his little circle used to compete with each other to show how much they'd read. I swear, by God, they only read so they could brag about it, so each one could show how much better he was than the others. Can you believe it, I'd sit with them, and at the end of an hour I'd know as much as they'd learned after days of reading. I didn't have time to read anyway. While they had their heads stuck in books, I was busy making small deals—though they weren't small then, not for a student like me. For a commission I'd tell the merchants about Faris, when he was due to come and the stock of provisions he was ordering for Barqais. Either the merchant paid me the commission or he didn't get to meet Faris. I was making as much as a university doctor earned, and more than what my old teachers earned. That's why I left university and joined Faris. I've taken whatever job he offered me. You can see the results for yourself, and you haven't seen anything yet."

He took a further sip from his glass.

"Look where Jalal is, and where I am! See where those books have got him, the books he stuffed his head with so as to be like all his friends. I wish he really would be like them. Some of them live a lot better than the wealthy people here—a thousand times better, by God Almighty! But Jalal and his comrades can't get hold of anything. All they ever want to do is moan how they've no money."

He paused, then got to his feet.

"They could make piles of money," he said, "if they only used their brains and had a little capital."

He stopped abruptly, as if feeling he'd said too much. Seeing her plunged deep in thought, he smiled.

This woman's Jalal's sort, he thought. If he'd married her, they would have spent all their time thinking, each in their own little world.

He found the idea comical, and let out a brief, cynical laugh. Drinking what remained in his glass, he felt drunk with self-satisfaction.

THREE

They Say the Guest's Your Brother

More than a year's passed since we had that talk, and I've said nothing more. As for Ihsan, he certainly never returned to the subject. He was busy with things I mostly knew nothing about. He started coming home from work very late, and he went off on several foreign trips.

For a year now I've waited for him to ask me to join in what he does, so I can shout and get angry, then stand my ground. But where once he used to get me involved in his game, now he's suddenly dropped me from it. Has he come to realize women in Barqais don't count in what men do? And has he learned that for himself or have other people explained it to him? It doesn't matter—the point is he's suddenly pushed me to the edge of his considerations, without even bothering to explain.

Every moment of this year I've dreamed, I've planned to rebel and reject, the moment that coiled person surges out from inside me. And then Ihsan would come gaily in as usual, embracing me, joking with me, all too often bringing presents for no reason. And then the revolt of that human person within would shrink and die down. Ihsan was happy, though he'd only tell me what he wanted to. There was a lot to tell, I realized that. But if I asked, he'd take no notice of what I'd said—just answer as he wanted.

He's changed a lot since that day—the day that man stormed in through the door, cutting off my enjoyment with the children, who silently dropped their things, sensing, as children do, that something big had happened. When he told the Asian maid to take them out, they trooped obediently off.

He came unexpectedly. Thrust the door open with his cane, and just walked in unannounced. Oh, if you could have seen al-Hemli's face! He was rooted to the spot, didn't know what to do. Then up he jumped, trying to welcome the man. But the man wouldn't sit down. Just said those three words: "I want Ihsan!"

Al-Hemli's face was rigid with terror! The project was still unsigned, and he had high hopes of sharing in our profits, relying on my help. Yet all he could say was: "As you wish, Your Highness."

Only then did His Highness sit down; and only then did poor al-Hemli get his breath back.

"Your Highness," he ventured to say, "if you'd just permit him to complete our current project—"

"Out of the question! I want his warranty transferred to me. Sign the papers by tomorrow."

He stood up, angry with Abdulrahman for his forwardness. His cane played over the Tabrizi carpet that covered the floor of the office. Then, all of a sudden, his manner changed—that man leaves me confused. His face became quite understanding and friendly. Meanwhile Abdulrahman stood there in front of him, silent and perplexed.

"He can work on with you—after the warranty's been transferred. For six months, in the afternoons, until you've completed the project."

With that he left as abruptly as he'd come. Al-Hemli went after him, trying to salvage something from the wreck.

"But the project, Your Highness. And the expansion of the dock. When will it be signed?"

The man gave a brief, sarcastic laugh at al-Hemli's attempt.

"Tomorrow you transfer the warranty. The day after you send Ihsan to me with the delegates."

After Ihsan went to work with His Highness, he became close-lipped about what he was doing. Even so, I realized the car agency wasn't their real aim. He might hold forth about it, with all kinds of details, especially in front of Faris. But he was holding something back, from me and everyone else, something to do with Jalal. One day he asked me gaily:

"Do you want Jalal to bring anything with him?"

I was stunned, and the delight on his face confused me too. Surely Jalal's coming wouldn't thrill him like this. I searched his face, but found no answer there. He looked handsome, though, a tall, slim knight—I have to admit it—more handsome than his brother perhaps.

"The formalities for his visit were finished today. But keep it secret. No one's to know about it."

I tried to put on a show of indifference. My voice obeyed me, and I became calmer.

"Could he bring some books?"

He moved from my side, and I couldn't see his face. Was he upset, or angry maybe? But there was no emotion in his voice.

"I can't ask him that—he'll be busy enough with other things for the moment. Ask him when he comes. Books!"

His cynical laugh boomed out. Then he disappeared behind the door.

Books! This woman, Ihsan, just doesn't realize what it is you're holding back from her. She'll never change, and she's incapable of understanding you. You get a kick, admit it, from the way she keeps trying to work out what you're doing—and you love her when she's jubilant, when she's confused, when she submits and you feel her fill your very veins and bones. But you won't keep her in the dark for ever; only until you've got what you want and you're sitting on the summit like a king, the way that fortune teller predicted. You'll tell her about everything, and you'll tell Faris and the others too. If Jalal will just act the way you want him to, the way he's always done. Then Nadia's going to swim in everything she could ever desire. What is it women want? That bedouin deputy summed up women's needs in a sentence, and his words traveled thousands of miles. Men of every sort saw the truth of it, talking of little else, until at last it reached Barqais.

His Highness recalled it suddenly and fell back laughing.

"Ihsan," he said, "what was it that deputy said, when they were debating women's rights in the parliament?"

It amazed him when you had no idea at all. He looked bloated, with the authority of a man entering a harem. His eyes glinted, then narrowed, and his trim beard danced as he laughed.

"May God guide you! Didn't you hear what he said? 'All a woman wants is a trailing gown, a bag spilling out stuff—and iron beating iron!'"

Is that what a woman means to them? So where does Nadia stand? How would they classify her? The bedouin deputy hadn't ever known a woman like that, so how could he distinguish one woman from another? You, Ihsan, can give them, and yourself, the first and the second, but you'd never consider the third. Leave that to Rashid, with his notions and his way of dealing with them. From the moment you started working together, you made that clear to him. Made it clear that you and Nadia are different, that other women don't come into your dealings—that you'll get on without having them take part in your game.

Since you started working for His Highness, you've made things clear to Rashid. You may be bound together in love of wealth and success, but each has his own ways and means of doing things. But that didn't stop him trying things on, competing with you. There you stood, like two fighting cocks in a ring, each proudly spreading his feathers, fierce and eager and wary—each so charged with hostility there had to be a confrontation.

His first attempt was when you were heading that Modern Car Company His Highness founded for you—your share thirty percent. You agreed without hesitation. You both knew it was just a screen for what you were planning.

"Lean meat" maybe—but not peanuts! You sold two hundred cars in the first deal, to various establishments and schools and institutes, and the same number to the police. And that was two months before you even got hold of the cars.

When Rashid came into your office, he was all friendly smiles, putting on a show to hide his resentment. He looked elegant with his silk shirt and gold watch, and his perfume came on ahead of him as he sat loftily down in front of your desk. You'd stood up, surprised to see him walk in unannounced. Then you remembered you should be sitting, so you sat down. He took out your card with the apology on it.

"I'm not," he said, "accepting a third apology to my invitation. It's beginning to look deliberate. It's highly embarrassing for me, in front of my guests, not to have you there. We're both working for the same man, after all! I don't want some of them imagining there's bad blood between us. Just come for an hour, then leave. The guests have all asked after you, both these last two times. They looked disapproving. What am I going to tell them the third time? Frankly, I don't like competitors to be continually talking about us."

You picked up your apology card and calmly tore it up. He watched as you did it, and his smile widened.

"Thank you, Mr. Ihsan," he said. "I'll expect you then."

When you went, you heard the raised voices, with their mixture of voices and dialects, even before the waiter led you through a back door of the Villa Rashid opening onto the garden. It seemed to you, for a moment, like a piece of land uprooted from some distant place and planted amid the sands. Lofty, aromatic jasmine and acacia trees, Dutch bulbs, with roses blooming around their stems, pruned by an expert hand. There were branches tastefully overhanging the walls and ponds, and three decorative palm trees gave proportion, spreading their arms and covering, with their fronds, lamps mounted above white columns, bundles of light scattering their shadows in inspirational forms. A temporary bar had been erected at the far end of the garden, beside the swimming pool which reflected the images of the guests crowded around it, plunged in their conversations and introductions. There were white robes, but these were almost lost in the abundance of European dress. It struck you Rashid had been watching for you. The moment he saw you coming through the door, he apologized to the person he was with and put his glass, brimming with drink and ice, on a silver tray carried by a broadly smiling Asian servant. Then, stretching out both hands in welcome, he conducted you to be introduced to some carefully chosen people. Then he paused, and you knew he meant to leave you for a time with the newly appointed engineering manager—a young man from Barqais who, in the face of all the fumes of drink and heavy smoke, spoke good English in quick, intelligent sentences that showed understanding. His talk was assured and good, though his eyes wandered constantly, seeking out light-colored faces and bare breasts and shoulders.

You tried to keep meeting his eyes with a show of interest. You were bored to tears. And you didn't miss the special look that passed between Rashid and that tall blonde woman as he passed her on his way to you. You saw the look again when, after waiting a little, she followed Rashid and he introduced you to her.

"Monsieur Natour—Danielle."

She was beautiful, with a clear complexion. Her eyes were sea-blue blended with a mossy green, her lower lip was marked with a red line giving it a plumpness irresistibly desirable. She was wearing too much of the same French perfume you give to Nadia; whichever way she moved, Nadia's smell engulfed you and you strove to control your desire. When Danielle spoke, the accent of her English revealed her French origin.

"Monsieur Rashid," she said. "Is our date for tomorrow still on?"

"Ten A.M., on the dot."

"Your garden's very beautiful, Monsieur Rashid. But your party would have been so much more fun if you'd invited us to put on bathing costumes and swim."

"If you were to jump in the pool as you are, Mademoiselle Danielle, I'm sure the guests would enjoy it. That would be marvelous!"

Ignoring his remark, she smiled at you. Her lower lip parted still further. She clung on to you, while the engineering manager devoured her with his eyes.

"Do you live here, Monsieur Natour?" she asked.

"Yes."

"I work for Air France, as a sales manager. I'm here on business, to expand our business and offices in Barqais."

Rashid deliberately went off. Pleading the need for a business talk, he put his arm in that of the engineering manager and led him off to a distant corner. The woman took on a more intimate air, her voice assuming a coquettish tone.

"The hotels here are so big. So splendid. But there's no alcohol. The Beach Hotel where I'm staying is as luxurious as any top hotel in the world. But it's so lonely."

You saw what she and Rashid were up to, and felt the urge to annoy her.

"Guests should abide by the laws of the country. Barqais holds on to its customs and traditions—it's a conservative kind of place."

Your gazes met over my glass. She didn't smile.

"Anyway, Monsieur Natour," she said, "my room's 701. I still have three long days."

She took something from her handbag, thrust it into your hand, then flashed a broad smile, revealing gleaming white teeth. She was desirable, captivating, but you had to resist. You opened her soft hand, put her card on it, then coldly closed the hand again.

"I'll be busy for some months to come," you said. "Enchanté, Mademoiselle Danielle."

She was still silently raging when Rashid caught up with you at the door.

"Ihsan. His Highness's sons are coming. Won't you stay a bit?"

Your eyes met. Two opponents who understood each other. You made an effort to sound jocular.

"Rashid. His Highness's sons are yours."

Then off you went without another word, triumphantly foiling Rashid's attempt to thrust women into your deals.

⮡

Faris too, since coming to Barqais, had realized the rules of the game. He'd succeeded without bringing women into it—and you, Ihsan, are still more lofty and unbending. Luck's all you need. With luck and nothing more the beads of good fortune can be set in place, and the locks to every door will spring open. Didn't luck blow, unexpectedly, in Faris's face? Jealous people say he meddled in things, put his nose into things, but remember the saying your grandmother and mother kept repeating: "Initiative breeds good fortune." Well, his initiative brought him face to face with luck. Dozens of times I've heard the story from Faris, and he seems to enjoy telling it more every time.

On closing its base camp operation, the company announced to its staff a formal auction to sell off used machines, cars, and radio and digging equipment. Faris had had no thoughts of entering the auction—in fact he hadn't even read the announcement. A client of his had mentioned the matter by chance, to show off his inside knowledge.

Faris had gone along at the due time, spurred on by curiosity and an urge to investigate. His car was speeding over the searing hot road when the two men saw him and knew well enough where he was going. According to Faris, they followed him in their own car, overtook him, then cut in, forcing him to stop. Their clean, spacious robes were perfumed with aloe-sticks, the scent wafting from them as a slight sea breeze sprang up from their direction. The road the three of them were on was quite empty except for their two cars. Faris insists he sensed something fishy the moment they stopped him. The camp was in sight now, and his keen instincts told him the sale had been rigged in advance and he had to be an expert hunter. One of the men opened the door of Faris's car and pulled him out.

"Everything's settled already," one of the men said. "You might as well go back."

Faris clapped his hands joyfully each time he reached this part of his story. His eyes would narrow, and he'd squint even more as his smile widened. "Man!" he'd say. "I could see something was up. I just stood there facing them."

"What do you mean, everything's settled?" Faris shouted. "This is a public sale, free for you, there for me. We'll see, shall we?"

The other man got hold of Faris's tie and pulled him closer. His fetid breath blew into Faris's face, like the stench of a stagnant pond.

"If you don't go back, you pimp," the man shrieked, "I'll smash your head for you! No one else is getting in here."

Faris had to fight off the smell, which his assailant's scented robes couldn't hide. He pulled the man's hand off his tie and thrust it down violently:

"Just try doing it," he said. "I'm going to tell everyone about you and the company—here and abroad. I'm going to complain to the government, and write to the foreign newspapers as well."

At this point Faris would laugh so much he'd lie back, lifting his feet right off the ground.

"The imbeciles!" he'd say. "I can't even write Arabic, let alone English."

The other man studied Faris's new suit and polished shoes, and his face dropped as low as his morale. Faris's acquaintances always teased him over his insistence on wearing a suit winter and summer alike. He, for his part, regarded it as a sign of class and an example to other people. His wife Afaf disliked the summer suit intensely, but it brought him some reflected esteem now.

He saw how the men had fallen silent.

"Come on then," he yelled. "Smash my head for me. I'd like to see you try."

The second man, disconcerted by Faris's nerve, pulled his companion away, then took Faris's arm and pressed it painfully.

"Man," he said. "*Salli annabi.*"

"*Allahoma salli ala sayidina* Muhammad," Faris replied.

"*Uthkor* Allah! We're Arabs—Muslims—brothers. Let's not behave like this."

"And do Muslims and Arabs go around waylaying people, the way you do?"

"Man—there's no harm done. *Uthkor* Allah."

Faris turned away, pretending to reflect.

"*Wanima billah—*"[8]

The first man, thinking his companion wasn't being tough enough, moved off and started kicking at the sand on the two sides of the concreted road. He looked at his gold watch, muttering loudly. The asphalt, stretching straight ahead, seemed to merge with the horizon, where, among the distant sands, the camp buildings had been planted like something from another country. The wind toyed with their baggy robes, the rustling lending a mournful touch to the situation.

"I'll be frank with you, my dear fellow," the first man said. "The whole thing's settled already. In fact, to be blunt, your little trip would be quite pointless. We've made an agreement with the official concerned."

Faris walked coolly to his car and opened the door.

"Why don't we all go and see?" he suggested.

The less aggressive of the two rushed to bar Faris's way. There was foam splashed around his lips, and suppressed hatred glittered in his eyes.

"Fifty thousand," he said, "and you go back."

Faris touched the few hundred in his pocket, then thought better of it and moved his hand out again. These staff members were thieves. He recognized them now— they'd come regularly to his photographic shops. Might it just be his curiosity was going to lead to a stroke of luck? He strove to control his beating heart and faltering tongue.

"A hundred thousand!" he said.

The other man stopped playing with the sand and spun around, his face congested with fury. His reddened eyes flickered and narrowed.

"Even the fifty thousand's too much," he said. "Do you think we pick up money off the street? Not a bizant more. Not another half dirham!"

The other man beckoned, while Faris pretended to reflect. He opened his car door and leaned on it, feeling that was the best way to control his trembling. Finally he said, in a firm tone: "In cash then!"

"We need the cash for the auction. We'll write you a check."

Faris sat down behind the wheel and made to close the door. The other man intervened.

"All right. In cash."

He took a black leather case from the back seat of their own car and began counting some wads of notes out loud. The case was crammed with similar wads.

Faris picked one of them up, and, just to spite them, counted it with apparent calmness. Then he opened his glove department, took out the contents and refilled it with the banknotes. Suddenly he started the car, causing the two men to leap back in alarm. Then off he went, waving merrily to them.

"Well done!" he shouted.

The car advanced a little, turned right around, then raced off, the tires screaming and scattering the sand. Faris was pursued by a volley of curses, lost in the breeze blowing from the other direction.

"You son of a bitch! You—"

With this fifty thousand Faris bought his first printing press, just as regular schools were being established through the country. School books, papers for ministries, invoices for shops. For three years, before anyone else in Barqais had thought of competing with him, his employees worked night and day, until he was loaded with money. He bought a new press after that, but, needing to get his money back from it, he founded a contracting company with his local partner, taking on four engineers, two European and two Arab. And so he'd become what he was today.

Faris had plowed a virgin land, and it had repaid him—wildernesses thirstily eager for drops of water they'd never known. But you, Ihsan, you're treading a land whose passion others have sucked already. They've worked on until they've drowned it, the options are narrowing. But, for all that, you'll make your summit, in a spot only you know of. With your own wit and Jalal's help.

Jalal. For over a year now you've worked to persuade him, to impress him in every sort of way. You've heard out his ideals for hours on end, until you were bored to death by him. All this time you've followed your plan, to convince him what you propose is for his sake, and the sake of his comrades and their ideals. You need his ideals and theories even so—they're the hammer you'll use, to knock on all the doors that are going to be opened for you.

✦

The VIP lounge at Barqais airport is quite spacious. The colors of the smart armchairs clash wildly with the sheen of Tabrizi silken rugs designed by expert hands, and with the numerous other pieces of furniture crowding the floor. Crossed golden swords hang facing the door, and the front part has a painting of the Shyoukh mounting a horse. The artist has taken pains to make the knight's face younger and more handsome.

As Ihsan entered with his greeting, the *fedewi*[9] gave an unusually warm welcome in return. Ihsan took a chair facing him, and neither said anything. Ihsan lit a cigarette, began smoking nervously. It irked him that the other man, for all the sudden respectful smile in his eyes, was watching him curiously. Ihsan had seen him several times in the reception room, whispering, bustling about, silently meeting the demands of his master. When told to leave the room, as happened very frequently, his face would show a lurking resentment. For that reason he'd seldom talked with

Ihsan, who glimpsed hostility in the man's eyes whenever His Highness and Ihsan talked privately together.

Since they'd met tonight, though, the man had been treating him differently. He'd hastened to greet him with open-eyed respect, letting him enter the lounge before him. Suddenly their eyes met.

"Ihsan," he said, "they say the guest's your brother."

Ihsan was elated by the inquiry. He answered slowly even so, striving to avoid either indifference or vaunting. "Yes," he said. "My blood brother."

That was an important distinction for these people. There were plenty of "brothers" in Barqais, countless from the father's side and a good many from the mother's.

"You know, Ihsan," the man went on, "your brother's comrades, they're real men—proper Muslims. God willing, they'll get the homelands back and bring pride to the whole Muslim and Arab world."

"God willing."

Ihsan felt a deep sense of satisfaction—the man was obviously repeating talk he'd heard at His Highness's assemblies. That meant they held Jalal in esteem and that they'd be ready to help him.

Tensely, Ihsan squashed the butt of his cigarette in the crystal ashtray before him. He stretched his legs, gaining a kind of pleasurable fulfillment from the likeness in the gleam of his silk socks and black shoes and that of the silken carpet. He gazed at the gold logo on the ends of the shoes, bearing the first letter of the famous designer's name. They're marks of status, Ibn Natour, he thought, and you have to keep them up.

The *fedewi* was slyly watching him. His kind know these shops and what they sell. They go into them to announce their masters' names, then stand around gathering up the numerous boxes with the shoes their patrons have chosen, mostly without even trying them on. If they decide later they don't like the shoes, or that the shoes are pinching their feet after the freedom of open sandals, then they'll fling them into closets for months or years on end, before they end up, finally, on the feet of their subordinates. Ihsan relaxed his back, aware of his tall stature.

"My father and grandfathers," he said, "were revolutionaries too."

The *fedewi* nodded as if to say he knew this, and went on eyeing Ihsan admiringly. Ihsan thought: Why did you let those words slip out? What are you trying to prove to him? He'll be impressed by the things he's heard from his superiors, about the tribes and their clans, and the lineages of horses and camels. He'll memorize old popular poetry too, eulogy, and verse about passionate love and war, which he's picked up in the nightly gatherings in his master's reception room. What does he care about any history you can lay claim to? There are plenty of jealous people coming here. They might decide to weigh things up, work things out, then throw out some innocent-sounding remark that's actually seething with malice.

His Highness wouldn't miss that. He'd open his eyes, realizing your grandfathers were like everyone else—that they'd lived in chains of ignorance and fear and simply given up. He'd know your father took part in demonstrations and strikes—but that real struggle in your family sprang up with Jalal. Be careful how you behave, Ibn Natour. The gulf between city-dwellers and bedouins may be vast, but the city-dwellers keep up their invasion, looking all the time for an ally or companion among the bedouins, seeking a fortune from this wealth that's sprung up out of the blue.

The *fedewi* rested his arms on his knees.

"Muslim countries," he said, gazing intently into Ihsan's face, "have always been coveted by godless people. There's been one invasion after the other. By God, Ihsan, I don't know why the Almighty doesn't destroy these people and get them off our backs! But no, brother—their country's beautiful, blessed with rain and wealth. Their women are immoral, their people are unbelievers. Whereas we acknowledge Almighty God, perform our religious duties. And look what happens—one disaster after another!"

He shook his head sadly.

"I tell you, Ihsan," he concluded, "Almighty God tests believers—we thank Him for the blessing of patience. He tests us so we return to sound and sane thinking—to unity and to know the taste of victory."

The loudspeaker announced the plane's arrival, and he jumped to his feet. Soon a smart black car stopped at the door of the lounge leading to the airport's small yard. The driver stayed sitting behind the wheel; and when the *fedewi* silently hurried to take his place alongside, Ihsan realized he was supposed to go and sit on his own in the back seat. He got in.

Jalal's tall figure appeared at the door of the plane. The hostess bowed to him, and the late night breeze ruffled his shirt, lending his wide shoulders a hugeness that seemed to narrow his hips and make them more graceful. The strands of his hair blew and gleamed as he walked down the steps, looking around to find someone—his questioning features recalling the curiously scared face, that day long ago on the mountain, when he'd turned to Ihsan, his pupils wide with fear, and said: "Nadia al-Faqih?"

The *fedewi*'s face assumed an expression of deep respect, followed by a fleeting disappointment as he noted Jalal's ordinary clothes. Curse your carelessness, Ihsan! You should have made it clear to Jalal how vital these small details are— you shouldn't have left it to him—you were too busy with the main matters—you were a stumbling horse, Ibn Natour. You should have remembered people here burnish the very grains of sand, that real glitter's lost in the tinsel glitter of husks.

With great respect, Jalal stretched out his hand to greet the *fedewi* standing there in his elegant clothes, in front of the grand car. But Ihsan rushed forward to prevent a disastrous confusion of which His Highness would surely have learned.

"Jalal!" he said. "His Highness is waiting to see you tomorrow."

Jalal's face clouded grimly as he realized the pit he'd almost tumbled into. As the brothers embraced, Ihsan whispered: "This is the *fedewi*—the guard. Don't be in such a hurry!"

The car sped over the empty city streets. The regular roar of the air conditioner added to the sense of desolation, as did the thorny shrubs alongside a road, without sidewalks, that seemed like black gravel. Ihsan eyed the speedometer and relaxed on finding the speed was no more than eighty. The *fedewi*, spurred on by memories and a desire to talk, turned around from the front seat.

"I tell you, Ihsan, and I don't care who hears it. The day the first plane ever arrived here, it landed on the water—it was before the old airport was built. People came out to see it. The women even mixed with the men that day. The whole of Barqais was there, old and young, right down to the babies.

We were all standing in the water. When it roared over our heads, we ran off, and the experts took charge. The old airport was built by the company when it came back here after the war. As for this present airport, the government built it just a few years back. You remember, Ihsan?"

"Everything starts small and grows with time," Ihsan said encouragingly. "Most of our Arab countries have small airports. Some don't even have one."

The exchange made the *fedewi* feel better. Suddenly he raised his legs and folded them beneath him on the luxurious seat.

"But the cars!" he went on. "If only you'd seen the first car! A Ford with a clutch, it was, they brought it for the senior sheikh, may he be in Paradise. It was red—beautiful, with an open top. There wasn't a soul who didn't go out and look at it. They lowered it at the harbor, and a Briton from the company drove it off. The Shyoukh gave orders for the car to be left for hours for the people to see. And whenever the Ford with the clutch passed through the streets, the children would chant and run after it. Today, by God's blessing, you see cars piled up in every house. May the blessing last. And may God protect our rulers."

Realizing from the driver's disapproving looks that he'd forgotten himself, he lowered his legs and stretched them out. Then he took his cigarette case and offered it to the two men, but both declined.

"Cigarettes are evil, brother," the *fedewi* said. "A curse. I started smoking the day the company came. Our fathers and grandfathers smoked a *gadoo*—what you call a *nargila*.[10] *Gadoo* at night, *gadoo* in the day, and not a single cough, for all the misery and toil, and the sea diving. These cursed cigarettes upset me, they clutch at my chest. But I can't stop smoking. You know, Ihsan, when the company came, all its foreign staff used to smoke. One Indian staff member used to collect the empty packs and put our wages in them. Rupees, brother. And he'd write our names on them. He used to exchange part of the salary for two packs, and so we kept on smoking. Just seeing a cigarette pack we'd be overjoyed, whether it was empty or full."

The car left the main road for a byway, and Ihsan realized they were heading somewhere different from where he'd been expecting. The *fedewi* stubbed out his cigarette in the ashtray alongside the driver, who was still evidently resentful.

They were entering a district of villas owned by His Highness. Half the villas he'd leased to the government as residences for high officials, allocated one to Rashid and left the other two for visiting guests.

"Jalal's staying with me," Ihsan said. He was resentful and tense. "At my house."

The *fedewi* didn't bother to turn around.

"Those are His Highness's orders," he replied. "He's to be his guest. The villa's ready. The appointment's tomorrow at four. After the afternoon prayer."

So it had all been decided in advance. Ihsan felt betrayed, felt that his status had been lessened in front of Jalal, who remained silent, uninterested in the words that had just passed, his lips parted in an ironic half-smile. Is he following your thoughts, Ihsan? That things aren't at your command the way you implied? That His Highness didn't tell you about having Jalal as his guest because he wanted you to know, from the start, that you're just an intermediary who doesn't count in his decisions? Or did he think you'd realize anyway, because he'd considered Jalal's visit important enough to propose it personally? You're worried either way, Ihsan.

Since I first learned he was coming I started preparing for the visit. I took out all the pieces of art stored away and adorned my house. I brought in some cleaners from Ihsan's office, and they polished everything. I chose a blue bedcover for the room he was to stay in, and blue curtains. I thought hard, then finally hung the painting opposite his bed, where he'd see it directly.

Before I bought the painting, I stood and gazed at it endlessly, while Ihsan shook his head and gave a mocking smile. A bolting horse galloping in a fog. And in the distance, where the painter had deepened his gray shades, was the quivering image of a mare, striving vainly to follow in the other horse's wake.

Ihsan inspected the elegant room and cast a fleeting look at the painting. Then, as he came out, he said: "Revolutionaries don't care about this sort of luxury, Nadia."

"He was a man," I said, "before he was a revolutionary. Actually, I think he has a deeper sense of beauty than most people have. Didn't he rebel, after all, for the sake of beautiful values? To change what's present and ugly? Is there anything more beautiful than freedom, Ihsan? And hasn't he rebelled to get it? How can he not have a sense of beauty, after he's worked with it until it burst out from him?"

He paused, then turned.

"Well then," he said, "you should have bought a natural scene from the country he loves."

"The land's a pretty narrow symbol for your country! The homeland isn't just earth and trees. If it were, a person would be attached to something merely tangible. A homeland's the mixture of sadness and joy on people's faces;

it's poverty and prosperity in mansions or tents; it's the stories of weary backs bending over the soil. Your country's the face of an old man—or the smile of a child attached to the land; it's the human beings, the farm beasts, the wastelands and the forests together—and the flowing of all these into your soul!"

He hesitated. Then a superior smile formed on his face.

"And what's the connection between all that and the horses in your painting? Are they national horses?"

His sarcasm didn't bother me.

"No, Ihsan. But you haven't tried to see the strange symmetry in the distances between the horse, the mare and the open space. And you haven't grasped the painter's fine sensibility in using that gray color."

He walked toward the hall, then said loudly: "You and Jalal don't know what it means to keep your feet on the ground. You don't live on it at all. You have your head in the clouds, both of you."

With that he banged the door behind him.

Jalal didn't go to the room I'd prepared. Ihsan was back by dawn. I'd fixed my make-up three times, perfumed myself lavishly, using quite an amount from the bottle, though it still seemed scentless to me! I moved things about, re-arranged them several times. What do I want from Jalal? Do I love him, or am I just a woman rejected and hurt once, trying to show him how life goes right on without him?

Time stood still as I waited. Suddenly, I recalled the scent of incense. What made me think of it? I got up, went to my cupboard and took out the bag I'd flung in there some months before. Then I busied myself burning incense in the gilded censer.

The house had been fragrant with great quantities of incense at that gathering at Her Highness's, the day I quarreled with Ihsan. I'd gone at the stated time, not knowing then that being a little late was a must in high society. The reception room was nearly empty, and she was sitting in the front part with her maid, while two servants stood at one end. The place was drenched in the scent of burning incense mixed with aromatic sticks. I told her how much I liked them, and she ordered that a censer be brought to me, though such a thing was quite against tradition. It was a silver censer adorned with designs in gold. Her Highness insisted I place it under my hair, then stand up. Soon she passed it between my feet, and the scent crept into my body. She laughed with those around her, imagining just where the scent had reached, then explained to me the difference between wood scents and fumes. My hostess was companionable, friendly, at that moment. Then, suddenly, she paused as some guests arrived. Her face took on a conventional, haughty air, and the visitors began showering her with false compliments, turning the place to heaviness and gloom.

As I left, a servant followed and handed me a bag.

"This is from Her Highness," she said.

I tried to return it, but her eyes glittered with anger and fear.

"It's not proper to refuse a gift," she said.

I took it hesitantly. There were women who'd left before me, or arrived after me, and no one had followed them. I felt a mixture of vanity and wonder at being singled out like that. Ihsan had no idea what I was carrying and waited curiously as I took out the contents of the bag—a gilded censer and a crystal vial filled with incense sticks. Ihsan had started the car.

"What made her give you that?" he asked.

"I praised it to her. Then the servant followed me with this."

As the car shot forward, he yelled out angrily.

"You shouldn't have shown your liking for anything in their place, no matter how beautiful it was. For them, expressing admiration's a way of asking for things. You should have known that, instead of letting yourself down."

"I'm not a beggar, Ihsan. I simply liked something and said what I thought about it. I wasn't expecting anything in return."

"Well, she understood it in her own way. Next time just don't say anything they might interpret the way they like to."

"To hell with you and their 'interpretations!' I'm not visiting her again."

I felt like bursting into tears, but managed to control myself.

"Listen, Nadia," he went on. "Either you learn to drive or I'll get you a driver. As for parking and waiting for you the way I did tonight—forget it!"

I stopped talking to him for two days. I threw the bag in my closet and forgot all about it. But that morning I started learning to drive.

I was shaded in a scented cloud when Ihsan came back, alone and furiously angry. His eyes gleamed with vindictive triumph as he sent his eyes wandering around the house, inspected my silk dress and saw my questioning looks.

"His Highness has asked Jalal to be his guest. Jalal's coming tomorrow to see the children."

Without another word he went off to his room. I felt so defeated I couldn't move. Pains suddenly struck my feet, from the pressure of the shoes I was wearing. I flung them off, one falling on top of an elegant crystal vase on the table in front of me, the other landing by the leg of the rosewood table. How had my clothes got so tight? I unbuttoned them, unbuckled my belt and curled up on the sofa in my silk dress, staring into space. The atmosphere was deadly oppressive.

When His Highness made that decision, he became my mortal enemy.

Jalal came. The moment he opened the door, before I saw him even, the blood began surging through the arteries in my neck, and a searing heat started glowing inside me, coloring everything around me. And as I caught sight of his tall form, all the bearings I'd plotted, to guide me at this moment, faded away. I was trembling, peering to see his face. Our eyes met for a brief second, then we both looked down.

He was the same young man who'd appear through the curtains, then vanish. Now, though, he had no choice but to walk toward me. I stood still. Was it the effect of the scorching heat that had reddened his eyes? He was still attractively tall in his casual clothes—the strands of his hair hung loose on his brow as I always imagined them. And he was trembling too. I searched to know with certainty what had left me baffled for so long. What was I to him?

But he couldn't look me in the eye as he stretched out his hand to greet me. His hand engulfed mine for a moment, then he blurted: "How are you, Nadia?"

It was a simple, unexpected question in that moment of awe, but it didn't make me laugh. I didn't know what to say either. In moments of turmoil you say senseless things in spite of yourself. Ordinary, simple things.

I realized my hand was staying too long clasped in his. I pulled it away abruptly and made a conventional reply.

"Thank God for your safe arrival."

Ihsan's face, it seemed to me, showed some anger as he noted our confusion. Then, acting with his usual speed, he ended the momentary agitation by putting his arm around Jalal, leading him to the sofa, then sitting opposite facing him. Jalal avoided even a stolen glance in my direction.

I forgot everything around me except for Jalal—the female within me awoke, happy at his agitation and seeking further certainty. I went and sat beside Ihsan, facing him.

Quietly and unexpectedly, Ihsan put his arm firmly around me, so that my head was touching his shoulder. Taken unawares, I felt my veins clogged with bewilderment and resentment, before the blood began painfully flowing once more. I looked at him. His face was congested, his palms clamped together as he silently reflected. Then the children rushed in to greet him, and his face relaxed a little as he busied himself with them.

Ihsan dropped the ice cubes into the whisky, slowly and with relish.

"Tell me, Jalal," he said. "Isn't Nadia more beautiful than ever, after marriage and having children?"

Jalal, startled, turned pale, then mustered a senseless smile. I watched him. He reflected for a second, then nodded in agreement, but didn't look at me. I had mixed feelings. I hadn't expected our meeting to be like this—but we both surrendered to what was happening. He took the glass from his brother, bumping it against the edge of the table as he brought it over.

What, I wondered, was Ihsan trying to do? Did he know of his brother's feelings toward me? Were they real feelings at all? I was puzzled, because Ihsan never says anything without some plan behind it. He passed me the orange juice with a smile, then embraced me once more.

Jalal tried to escape from the situation.

"Do you still read, Nadia?" he inquired.

"Sometimes. But there aren't too many new books here. Not good ones."

"Just think, Jalal," Ihsan broke in sarcastically. "She wanted you to bring her some books. I didn't tell you that, did I?"

Jalal was furious at this.

"You should have told me. Why didn't you? I could have got you any number of books. I'll send them on later. I've been reading a novel by a Sudanese novelist. I'll send it to you."

As he continued, I hung on his words.

"In the novel the writer discusses relations between north and south—the reaction to expatriation—the hero tries to overcome his alienation through sex in the developed society of the north—he tries to conquer his feelings of loneliness in bed—but the north, represented by his British woman, won't recognize his expatriation or fuse with the south—"

I searched in his words to find exactly what he meant. Was that the last book he'd read? Or was he reminding me of my own alienation? Should I put some weighty interpretation on his words, when he was maybe just talking at random to cover his confusion?

Soon, though, he regained his calm composure, talking about neutral things.

"Nadia—are you—all happy here? This is a strange kind of city, endless streets with nothing but cars, sidewalks without anyone walking on them. It's a city without any clear character, not clean, not dirty, buildings and walls hiding everything. Can a person really be happy here?"

These moments while he talked, short though they were, allowed me to regain a measure of composure.

"Don't you think, Jalal," I said, "that happiness is a state of mind, and that you could be happy being alone? What's special about life in Barqais is the way it gives you a chance to choose, to pick out the friends you want. When you're in a foreign society, nobody's forced on you."

Ihsan, not liking my drift, brought our discussion to a close.

"Nadia's happy," he said, "because she's with me."

Any chance to answer or carry on with the talk was spoiled by the ringing of the doorbell. In rushed Afaf, with Faris behind her. She flung herself on Jalal and embraced him, weeping aloud. That woman puzzles me. She cries, laughs, writes worthless poetry, all with total simplicity. Faris eventually put an end to the lengthy embrace, but still she showered her brother with smacking kisses.

Faris sat down and, from a silver basket set on the table in front of him, took a piece of chocolate. He unwrapped it and devoured it with relish, then moved to the edge of the sofa, getting ready for a second piece.

"Do you see, Jalal?" he said. "There's nothing in this country except work, food and sleep."

He laughed, winking at his wife, and she laughed in her turn, then thought better of it and blushed with embarrassment, remembering she was in the presence of her brothers. Faris went on.

"As for your sister, sir, she's still writing poetry. Sheets and notebooks of it. Imagine! She even flirts with sand, insisting her inspiration comes better on the beach. To hell with inspiration like that! Man, I'd be half dead from the scorching heat and humidity, while my dear wife was waiting for inspiration. Ha, ha! By Almighty God, I could be striking a hundred deals while she's watching the sunset and the tide going in and out. It's okay, I'd say, she's just one of Adam's ribs, ha, ha. One day your sister felt the urge to write. Faris, I said, you go closer to the sea, where inspiration might come out of the water. Another meter and the car was plunging down into damp sand. Aah! I cursed the sea, and poetry, and anyone who obeys a woman. Three hours we walked that night, with no one in sight. Then at last a beach cruiser passed, and after endless questions they finally got us back. That day I vowed I'd stay away from the sea. Poetry be damned! Well, you're the blessing and the revolution now. Afaf's abandoned the sea and the sand and the birds—what she writes about now is the homeland and revolutionaries. Would you like to hear her latest poem?"

None of us paid any attentiom to what he'd been saying. As for Afaf, she remained silent. Faris devoured a third piece of chocolate and wiped the spittle from his mouth.

The glimmer of recollection flickered in Jalal's eye. I glimpsed it as he asked: "Are you still fond of chocolate, Nadia?"

"Sometimes."

I could feel the chocolate in my hands. I was returning home at night, and he was standing in front of their door. He walked behind me for a few steps, then put two bars of chocolates in my hand. "This is for you," he said. Then he was gone, without another word. I stood alone, trembling.

The women had gone to congratulate his mother, who was celebrating the birth of the baby born to Faris and Afaf, and my mother had insisted I go with her, as mothers always do, because "Um Jalal[11] has two eligible young sons." Jalal came into the room as we were alone there with his mother. He offered me some sweets, but I shyly refused.

"Have a piece," he said. "Don't you like it?"

"No. I prefer chocolate."

It was just something that came into my mind, to hide my confusion—and there he was waiting for me with the chocolate. I kept the bars for three weeks, but then, the first time he avoided me, I ate the first bar. When it was finally clear he'd stopped taking an interest in me, I ate the second.

Faris scooped up a handful of chocolates. He offered one to his wife, but she turned her face away, and Jalal declined too. He seemed bored with everything going on around him.

"You know, Jalal," Faris said, "when we first came to Barqais, chocolate was something you only dreamed of. Man, I swear by Almighty God, Ibn al-Hazimi was the only one who ever got any, from Jerusalem—his cousin's one of your people—you know him—one of the big shots—from Jerusalem."

Jalal nodded silently.

"This Hazimi was one of the first engineers to come to Barqais. His family lived in Beirut, and his mother used to send him loads of chocolates, as if that was the only thing we needed. Ha! He slept, along with his colleagues, in a room with a roof made of reed and wood. It only had one air conditioner, and he'd stuff the chocolates in the vent."

Reaching this part of the story, Faris lay back and laughed.

"His colleagues used to eat the chocolates and stuff pebbles in the wrappers instead. Ha, ha! That gave me an idea. I imported chocolates four times a year, for Muslim and Christian feasts, to supply the company's foreign employees. The second year I doubled the quantity, the third year I trebled the quantity and price together, but it all spoiled. It got maggot-ridden, and I lost my money. It's difficult to store chocolates, man, they spoil too fast. So I said, to hell with all that stuff only the grandees eat. Ha, ha!"

Faris, that drum stuffed with money, missed out on learning the law of craving and the need for satiety. Busy piling up money, how could he have read what Kazantzakís said through his Greek hero?[12] Isn't everyone that Greek child who craved the cherries he couldn't afford to buy? The only way he could assuage his craving was to steal money and buy a basket of cherries, which he devoured voraciously until his stomach revolted and he had to throw it all up in a ditch.

Ihsan and Jalal had started fidgeting, and it tormented me I was losing my chance amid all this nonsense. Ihsan put an end to the situation by laying down his empty glass and saying: "You've so much to do, Jalal. We have to prepare the report His Highness asked for. It's getting late."

Neither of us had expected this, and Jalal seemed resentful, though he made no objection. Faris and Afaf said goodbye and left. I stood up as if to apologize, and neither insisted I stay.

༺❧༻

I spent the next two hours lying forlornly on my bed, not knowing what I wanted. Then I heard them start arguing loudly. Driven by a curiosity I couldn't resist, I sneaked out ,and stood in a place where I could see inside the living room. Jalal had his back to me, while Ihsan was leaning against the bar with an angry air. I didn't mean to eavesdrop. Even so I went on standing there, longer than I should have done, knowing—

"Listen, Jalal," I heard Ihsan say. "I'm doing this, first, second and third, for the cause. For more than a year now I've been trying and trying to convince you of that. But this four percent is my right—if you don't suggest it tomorrow, I'll be lost. If you could only see the way the rest of them treat these people. Like a saw—up they gain, down they gain. And you think your own brother isn't worth four percent!"

Jalal got up and casually put his hands in his pockets. As he turned, I moved aside. Then I heard his voice, calm and indifferent.

"I'm going now. His Highness's driver must be turning gray, he's been waiting so long."

Ihsan was seething with annoyance.

"Not before I've convinced you. You can't ruin everything I've built up. For me, four percent, of the total— then six percent divided between us, three for you and three for our company. Here they are, crying out for arms, while you get hold of them so easily you're just piling them up. They don't have any relations with the socialist countries, and they need something from there. I'm the middle man, and I don't think taking a commission clashes with ideals or nationalism. No other broker would have agreed to less than ten percent of the whole thing. It doesn't conflict with the welfare of the country. It's my country too, have you forgotten that?"

Jalal headed for the door without a word. Ihsan called beseechingly after him.

"Jalal, please—tomorrow's my last chance. Explain things to them. You wouldn't let me lose my share, would you?"

Jalal opened the door, paused, then turned to him.

"Our share, Ihsan. You'll take two percent and no more. The other two are for me—of the total!"

༺༻

Nadia gave a start as, with a dramatic gesture, Ihsan laid the envelope down in front of her. Her hand shot up, making her book snap shut. She read her name printed in English on the elegant envelope, but made no attempt to reach out for it.

What's going on in this woman's head? Nothing you do, Ihsan, ever dazzles her or impresses her. Why has she kept to herself since Jalal's visit, and almost stopped seeing him? Even this huge house you've moved to now doesn't make her happy.

She'd hung the painting of the horse in the living room and taken to sitting in front of it for long periods.

"Wouldn't it look more beautiful," she'd asked him suddenly, "if the painter had turned the mare's head and made her gallop off in the other direction?"

"Have you forgotten she's a female? The rib of a male?"

She ignored the labored joke.

"If the painter had done that, the mare would have left the horse's sphere, we would have seen what she looked like. In the end she would have come out from that gloomy gray."

Again she ignored his laugh, and went on talking to herself.

"But the painter reversed the reality. The mare should have turned her neck, of her own accord, run off in another direction. That way she would have freed herself from the gloom and the horse's shadow."

She got straight up, took the painting from the wall, then called the Asian maid.

"Take this," she told her. "You can have it. Hang it in your room if you like."

The maid just stood there in amazement, unable to understand.

"Nadia," Ihsan said, seeing the envelope still untouched, "don't you want to know what's in the letter?"

Slowly she turned the envelope around, but still didn't open it. Exasperated, he took it from her, opened it and handed her the letter.

Mrs. N. Natour (it read),

We have deposited in your account gold to the amount of two hundred thousand dollars at the rate of five American dollars per gram.

Sincerely yours,

Banque Crédit Suisse, Zurich.

He searched her eyes for the joy glittering in his own, but found none.

"Who said I wanted gold?" she said.

"Who turns gold down?"

"For a sum like that I'd rather have land."

What was happening deep inside this woman? What did she really want?

"Land, rather than gold? Gold lasts better. Besides, the price is expected to treble in the next few months. Land! How much of it do people have left? If it hadn't been for my mother's gold, we would have been beggars after the emigration. Next time, as a matter of fact, I'm buying the same amount of gold for the children."

"I want land," she said bluntly.

"Look, half the women in the world couldn't even dream of having what I've given you. Nothing impresses you! At least smile, say thank you. Gold's already started rising, today, and it's set to double over the next week, then treble. It could even go higher, and quicker than you think. How much is the price of land going to rise, tell me? And you'd still rather have land than gold?"

"Isn't gold a blessing from the earth, Ihsan? Would you ever have owned the gold if it hadn't been for the land?"

What does this woman know? What does she mean anyway? She hasn't the least idea of what you've done or what you're going to do. Just words!

He pulled viciously at the letter, but she clung on to it. It almost tore.

"I'll sell the gold," he said. "Then, later on, I'll buy you— land."

"No, buy me that from the next deal. I'll keep the gold."

"No, Nadia, gold or land. One of the two."

"Both, Ihsan. The two together won't come to ten percent. That still leaves you nine tenths of the total. As of now, and until you've done it for me, we sleep in separate bedrooms."

She turned back to her book, while he stood there, gaping at her in disbelief.

FOUR

So Why Are You Trembling?

It's true that wealth's sweet, Ibn Natour! When the big shots enter the game, the parts get played to perfection, and the show gets grander and more dazzling still.

The Barqaisi embassy car left Heathrow Airport and passed through a small gate, with the letters VIP printed on a blue board. Its British driver was in his early fifties, but smart and erect.

Things are moving faster and easier than you ever thought, Ihsan—so much easier it seems unreal! It's less than two months since you visited Rashid Salman in his office, and now he's phoned you, his voice jubilant with triumph.

"You can come in two days, Ihsan, and sign the necessary papers—everything's fine—we'll need a week in London, then another in Paris."

You couldn't believe your ears. And you were thinking of her.

"Shall I bring Nadia along?"

Rashid's laugh, booming into your ears from the distant city of fog, brought you right down.

"No, no! Not Madame Nadia. It's still early."

A quiver passed through you, as you felt the softness of

her body rushing warmly into your blood. She's never been so bent on depriving you of her nearness as she is now. She knows you desire her, and she makes you suffer by refusing you. Nadia al-Faqih! How she's changed. And how self-possessed she's become!

And yet her cruelty inflames your desire. And now this donkey insists "It's still early." What does he know of your suffering?

Rashid offered him a cigarette. He took it, then busied himself watching the rushing crowds and lines of cars that block London by five in the evening.

"The weather's been wonderful for days here," Rashid remarked.

Ihsan said nothing. Rashid went on.

"I hope it stays like this. That way we'll have sunshine to celebrate the new office."

This man knows how to amuse himself with small things, so as to hide what he's planning. He's good, though, even abler and cleverer than I thought. When you decided to have him in your game, as a mere secondary player, you were sure he'd be able to help you, stop you wasting effort and money and time. That's why you asked to see him two months ago.

He came out of his office some minutes after you'd arrived. That, you realized, was deliberate—his secretary had seemed embarrassed, finding pointless things to do, asking you to wait just a moment, even though she knew who you were. You went in. His desk was almost bare—just a box of cigarettes, an ashtray and files impeccably stacked. Everything in his office was grand. You liked his fine taste—the gilded Louis XV desk, the cabinet in the same style, with its collection of antique pieces. The two armchairs, blue as the sea, were in total harmony with the silk carpet beneath them.

You let your attention be taken by the figure of a woman in rose-red jasper, her body like the lower part of the Sphinx. A squatting lioness against her arms, her tresses flying as if blown in a storm, spreading like a sail, as she gazed proudly, haughtily into the distance. What was the sculptor trying to say? Unconsciously you walked toward it. On the base of the statue was mounted a small yellow plaque, with the signature "Salvador Dali."

Dali, Picasso, Angelo, impressionism, cubism, surrealism—to hell with the lot of them! You weren't listening when Nadia tried to stuff your head with them during your first visit to Paris, a few months back. Rashid's clever with that sort of thing. No doubt being on top of luxury, knowing the various aspects of art and prestige, are part of the game.

There was still a long line of people in front of you, and she was waiting excitedly. In front and behind were young men with long hair and unwashed bodies, burning to see the miracle. You tried to see what it was they were seeing— an ordinary woman with plump hands—and Nadia stood motionless in front of her. Someone behind her was protesting loudly.

"Nadia," you said, "if this woman had walked in front of a battalion of men, none of them would have taken any notice."

She got heated up, started shouting, talked about the woman's mystical smile that had baffled the world, about the artist who'd created her. It was shameful, she said, when people didn't appreciate art and the beauty of art. You started apologizing—and that remark of yours cost you more museums, and churches, and tombs, and mummies.

You'd wanted the Lido, the Pigalle, the café at the George V hotel, to joke about what you'd seen to people visiting His Highness.

But Rashid knows both sorts, he's master of both games. That's why you had him play a part in your plan, if only a limited one, so you could learn from him.

"Rashid," you told him, "I want to found a company for general trading. Headquarters in London, with branches in Paris and Greece. I want to incorporate it and establish bank accounts."

Rashid's smile widened, but he said nothing.

"I'll call it the JANA General Trading Company."

You made a blend of their two names: Jalal and Nadia. It was to please Rashid, and to be a good omen for you, because you've been rising ever since you married her. Your father, God rest his soul, kept warning you against pessimism. But you can't help being the two together—pessimist and optimist!

The car rounded Trafalgar Square, where Nelson still stood grandly on top of his column, surrounded by lions spouting water from their mouths. There were crowds of people milling about, and pigeons pecking at grain, even though dusk had fallen.

As the driver halted before a tall building overlooking the square, Ihsan realized the extent of the surprise Rashid had in store for him. The driver opened the door for Rashid, but without bowing, then moved quickly toward Ihsan, who regretted now that he'd already, in his haste, unconsciously opened the door and got half way out of the car, to the astonishment of the driver and Rashid's superior amusement.

"You should have waited, Ibn Natour," he said, "for the driver to open the door. You haven't mastered that yet.

It's one of the tokens of prestige."

The effusive porter, wearing a neat dark suit, was behind a desk, small and elegant, that went well with the lobby's decor of wood and plaster. There were plants in pots spaced artfully around the lobby, and a painting was hanging between two armchairs.

The porter bowed slightly.

"Good evening, Mr. Salman," he said.

He straightened, then added: "Good evening, sir."

"This is Mr. Natour," Rashid said. "The manager."

The porter, bowing, greeted him once more. They left the elevator at the fifth floor, then walked along a carpeted corridor until they were in front of a door displaying a splendid glittering plaque that said: "JANA General Trading Company."

Rashid spread his arms in a dramatic gesture.

"Welcome to your offices, Mr. Natour!"

With that he conducted him through a medium-sized room with very elegant leather furnishings.

"This is the secretary's room."

This led on to a grand, spacious office. The walls were paneled in gilded white wood. A green granite fireplace was built into the front part, and within its hollow was a crystal chandelier adorned with semi-precious yellow and mauve stones, which sparkled splendidly when Rashid pushed the light button. Power is sweet, Ibn Natour, Ihsan thought. God rest the soul of the coal-burner in those first days after the emigration, then the Boori wood burner when things had got easier—

The office furniture was all in harmony: the desk, the leather easy chairs, the small table for meetings at the far end. The curtains the color of pistachio nuts and the decorative pot plants made a captivating general effect. Rashid pulled a folding door, which opened onto a board room capable of holding a general meeting, its chairs upholstered in blue velvet.

"This was the headquarters of the Australia Trading Company, Ihsan. Then an American trading company like yours offered to buy it. But I had a talk with the broker. I offered him fifty percent more and clinched the deal."

"Splendid."

Gazing from the board room window, Ihsan saw the whole of Trafalgar Square spread out in front of him. A group of musicians with long hair and tattered clothes began playing a delightful tune, and people quickly clustered around them. On the other side, on the building directly opposite, he saw the neon sign for Middle East Airlines. How much of that last fifty percent went to Rashid, Ihsan? Well, never mind. Jalal's instructions had been clear: open an office in London, and another in Paris, and incorporate the company in your name and the name of His Highness.

"We've done as you asked," Rashid said. "There's a finance manager doubling as accountant, a clearing agent and an office manager acting as a secretary for you too. As for legal matters, they'll be taken care of by a top-class lawyer's office in the building opposite ours."

Ihsan nodded, his eyes following two lovers moving from the square into a side street. Both were wearing blue jeans and baggy shirts, and their hair was the same length. Only the young man's broad shoulders marked him out from his companion.

What, he wondered, went on in these people's minds? How could they forsake every kind of beauty for such dissolute bohemian ways? Does this freedom from all bonds, Ibn Natour, realize some absolute beauty of which you know nothing? No. No, they're just crazy! They can't know the world contains such elegance and luxury as you have—and there's more to come.

"The concierge will see to cleaning the office."

Ihsan turned to him. Rashid realized he hadn't understood.

"Sorry. I mean the porter—the concierge."

He pronounced it, this time, with a marked accent. This Rashid, Ihsan thought, gets people's favor and admiration because he knows things. His Highness and his sons need his services, at home and abroad, because he speaks French and English so fluently.

"You mean the same porter, Rashid? The one in the hall? The smart young fellow behind the desk?"

"Yes, after he's finished that work, he has a contract with the company to clean the whole building. I think he's the best person for the job."

Ihsan was still in a state of amazement as they went back into the secretary's room. Rashid took a card from a small box on the table and gave it to Ihsan: On the card was printed "JANA General Trading Company," and there were three telephone numbers plus another for the telex.

Rashid's so thorough, he thought. Well, this devil's welcome to what he takes from you.

"Tonight, Ihsan, I've invited the staff to dinner in your honor. It seems to me work at JANA will need a special kind of bond, a family atmosphere. Don't you think so?"

He turned toward the door, then added: "We have to be off to the hotel now. We don't have much time."

He could hardly refuse.

"All right," he said irritably, following Rashid. "Though frankly I would have preferred meeting them in business hours."

༺❦༻

Throwing himself onto the bed in his room at the luxurious Grosvenor Hotel, Ihsan still felt depressed. He took one drag on his cigarette, then stubbed it out with an irritable gesture. For all the elegance around him he was lonely, and the image of Jessica Raban kept haunting him.

Why are you afraid of her, Ihsan? Because Rashid chose her? He chose the others too, didn't he? Mr. Black, the finance manager, who seized every chance to show how much he knew. He didn't say a lot, but he chose each word with care. And Mr. Wright, the lawyer, loftily listing some of the big companies he represents, along with hints about some big houses he'd bought for men from Barqais. You were impressed by all that. After all, you need to talk to him about the deals made in the office, as a cover for what you're doing behind the scenes.

So why, Ihsan, are you comparing your feelings about Mr. Black, and Mr. Wright, with your feelings toward Jessica Raban? Is it because she's a woman? Or is it her self-assurance and wit?

Jessica Raban, the office manager. Body tiny and slim, a beautifully tanned complexion. Thin lips painted in a transparent crimson, making her eyes gleam like honey. Long hair, not blonde, not chestnut either, curled in a bun behind her small head. She could come from any of the countries north or south of the Mediterranean. And then, her white silk dress, showing fine taste.

Even as she shook hands with Ihsan, she was looking him confidently in the eye.

"Tell me, Miss Raban," Ihsan said, "why did you leave your last post?"

"Because when you bought the offices, Mr. Natour, the old company's headquarters were moved to New York."

"And what were you doing before that?"

"I had my own office. Real estate."

He chuckled derisively as he attacked the steak the waiter had set in front of him.

"Women? In real estate? I suppose the office went bankrupt and the company closed it?"

Blood oozed from the steak, mixing with the sauce. He lay his fork down abruptly, and their eyes met. Hers held a mixture of pride and anger.

"Quite the reverse," she said. "I can assure you, Mr. Natour, our profits surpassed all expectations. Actually, love was the reason."

Rashid called the waiter and told him to change Ihsan's rare steak for one that was well done. Ihsan, though, was following her next words intently.

"As I said, love. My female partner fell in love with one of our clients and moved to Geneva, where he lives. She lost all interest in the company. After that I didn't feel able to go on alone. We'd studied together at school, then worked for a while in a real estate office. We learned a lot there, started our own office, and things went well. But when she got married, I really didn't feel like working on without her—I sold the office and came to work for the Australia Trading Company. So you see, Mr Natour, it was my love for her, and her love for her husband, that was the reason."

Rashid pitched in, making heavy use of his knowledge of French.

"Well, working with Mr. Natour will be something exceptional. *Très unique. Intéressant.*"

"Tomorrow," Ihsan said, trying to change the subject, "we'll start our shipping of Jaguar motors and spare parts, first to Athens, then on to Barqais. I think, Mr. Black, you'd better be in Athens by the end of next week." He was reassured and pleased to find no one opposing the idea.

Something about Jessica, though, still puzzled him, in spite of the things she'd told him about herself. Opening his leather briefcase, he took out a book entitled *Learn French in a Week.*

"Bonjour—bonsoir—ça va bien? Merci beaucoup. Mon Dieu!"

He dialed a number on the phone.

"Nadia?"

Her voice was sleepily surprised. He made a mental calculation. It was dawn in Barqais.

"Sorry to disturb you, Nadia. Tell my secretary to call the French Cultural Center tomorrow. When I get back, I absolutely must have a French teacher. Even if they have to bring him in from Paris—"

Her superior laugh hurt him.

"Shall I send him now? When you woke me up, I thought it must be something urgent!"

She'll never understand what you're going through, or what you're trying to achieve. But you love her, Ihsan. She knows that, and she uses it to torment you.

༺༻

"Miss Raban. Could you come in right away?"

Her dress was elegant, her make-up light and flawless.

Her face relaxed as she saw his smile.

"Jessica, I want you to buy me a house, in London or Paris. How long would it take you to clinch a good deal— on your own account?"

She couldn't conceal her astonishment, remembering the eccentricity of some of her previous clients. Then she smiled.

"No doubt," she said calmly, "any good deal for JANA is a personal success for me."

"No, no Jessica. I'm not talking about JANA. I'd like to invest your knowledge of real estate in a secret I hope you'll keep to yourself."

She was curious but wary.

"Jessica, my wife's birthday is two months off. I want to give her a house, here or in Paris. She's a sensitive woman, and refined."

There was a special glow in his eyes, which Jessica understood. His feelings were obvious, and she smiled tenderly. The revelation lessened the distance between them, and Jessica had a comfortable air now, an encouraging smile widening around her white teeth.

"For what sum, Mr. Natour?"

"If you can find the right house, the price doesn't matter."

He gave her the files about the Jaguar company, along with the staff files, and she went out.

He took out her own file and flicked over a number of pages. Jessica Raban, born in Lyon, studied in France, completed her studies in Geneva, then worked in London. But still, he thought, there's something puzzling about this woman.

He stretched his legs over the elegant desk, and, as he looked through the window, his gaze struck the wall of the building opposite. Would Nadia appreciate what he

was doing? Well, his biggest deal was coming, and Athens
wasn't too far off.

~≈~

We've been waiting for four days. Ihsan's been very tense,
anticipating something big. It was clear enough to me, but I
didn't ask him, and he said nothing. There was a volcano
inside him, bursting out of the calm of Glyfada—this wealthy
Athens suburb on the Greek coast, which gets quieter in
early June. I can feel his rage as he jumps into the water, as
we go sailing to the small islands, or stop for a while in front
of the potter, or mix with the crowds of tourists.

I didn't argue when he suggested spending a few days in
Greece, before going on to London. He'd chosen, he
claimed, to come to Glyfada, a small, luxurious place—big,
quiet villas with the waters of the Mediterranean at their
corners, at the foot of a mountain, with nothing to disturb
it except the waves lapping on the sands and the drone of
planes at the nearby airport. Ihsan demanded we stay there
alone, and he sent the children off to a summer school in
Geneva to learn English, music, and horse riding. "Nadia,"
he said, "they ought to be brought up differently." I'd read
some leaflets about the school. It was a completely different
world, and I agreed.

For four days I've been waiting for something
extraordinary to happen, here in this distant place. I've
fantasized, had dreams of him coming from nowhere—
welling up out of the sea, or the mountain, or the road.
I had no idea what I wanted from him. I just wanted to see
him, face him, to know why he'd changed. Where's that face
everyone used to know? Jalal, the father of principles and

ideas. Why did I have to hear what he said? Did I somehow misunderstand him? Why? Was he trying to take revenge on Ihsan, or was I just a number in his calculations? Has he really changed?

I don't know how it happens that wishes come true sometimes, by some unknown force akin to miracle. After just four days he came. We were in a far corner, sitting by the hotel pool under a shady pine tree. The sea was spread out in front of us, with a paved road between, plus the extension of the narrow sandy beach. The waiter bowed and said: "Mr. Natour. Mr. Gonzales is here."

Ihsan shot out of his seat. As for me, the visitor was no concern of mine, and I kept my eyes on my book until he called my name. It was him! Jalal Natour, alias Mr. Gonzales!

The elegance of his summer clothes, with the designer logo on one of the pockets, couldn't hide the several kilos of weight he'd put on. For all the shock and impact, I glimpsed his plump chest. He'd grown a short mustache and swept back his soft hair. Seeing how confused I was, he stretched out his hand toward me.

"Disguise is part of our lives, Nadia," he said. "Security reasons."

"Gonzales—Gonzales—"

I realized I was endlessly repeating the name. Why was I so deeply shocked by something I'd been wanting to happen for so long? Every single moment I'd been wishing he'd come, emerge from the incredible, that I could glimpse him in the unexpected. So why did his presence shake me so? I wasn't as jubilant as I thought I'd be. Since I'd heard them talking that time, he wasn't like my image of him any longer. More than two years had passed since he allowed himself to change—or rather, since I saw that unfamiliar face of his.

I realized, the moment he came, how I wanted him to appear, just to see my face—to know how I've changed—how I've come to possess myself. How this inner person deep inside me has become taller, grown up, learned to attack with strength every now and then. It's still inclined to sleep, but when it does wake, I rebel, quarrel, impose—and Ihsan submits to me.

I love and fear this great rebellion within me. Yet I don't know where to direct it, or where it would take me if I unleashed it.

~❧~

For the first time since I'd known him, I found his hand plump and extremely soft. He held my own hand tightly, keeping it in his.

"You're as beautiful as ever, Nadia," he said. "That color really suits you."

I was wearing a rose-red cotton dress. My black hair was held with a white band, my white sandals adorned with rose-red beads. I was simply but elegantly dressed that day—I'd learned to be my own judge as to my appearance. I'd bought the dress from a shop in the Champs Elysées. The salesgirl had asked me, in competent English: "What's your star sign?"

There were crowds of people surging all around us, coming in, going out, being taken up and down, in the electric elevators, from the first floor of the Lafayette Gallery. I was happily entranced, and Ihsan was selecting some neckties. I tried two perfumes on my wrists. Ihsan smelled them carefully, then chose the one I was hesitant about.

"This one suits you better," he said.

I asked the salesgirl for two bottles of it.

"Madame."

Her voice was as sharp as her features.

"What's your sign?" she asked.

Not understanding why she was so curious, I said nothing. After some time, she asked: "Are you a Pisces? I'm sure you are."

I was taken aback by her angry tone. But she was right. I nodded.

"No wonder you submitted to him," she scolded, the anger glittering in her eyes. "Pisces people are always easily led. You even let him choose your perfume! People born under Pisces are fatalists and dreamers. They're afraid of making changes and decisions."

Ihsan, listening happily, answered her in his half-mastered French.

"She does that, mademoiselle," he said, "because she loves me."

"Rather, monsieur," she answered, "because Pisces people opt for peace and security."

"I reckon she's a Pisces who's disappointed in love," Ihsan said sarcastically, in Arabic. "Someone jilted her, and now she's smarting under her bad luck."

He put his arm around me, then asked her: "How about you?"

"Me?" she said, angrily handing him our purchase.

"What does it matter? As long as I'm not prepared to give in?"

Ihsan was still laughing as the elevator took us up. The things we'd bought were getting heavy now, and Ihsan stopped to buy a suitcase.

On the third day after our marriage, Ihsan happened to

spill the contents of my suitcase, then tried to help me sort them. Most of the things were rose-red, my favorite color.

"I don't like rose-red," he said. "I don't want you to wear it."

"But it's my favorite color."

"Well, I hate it. Don't you wear things to please me?"

I became the daughter of that Arab woman who repeated her mother's advice on her wedding night. For a whole year we'd sat on the wooden steps in front of our teacher, repeating what the Arab woman had pronounced. "Fall in with everything he commands."

Then there was the thing our neighbor in Damascus told me, when she came to wish me goodbye before I joined Ihsan in Barqais.

"I tell you, Nadia, if I couldn't find something to decorate my hair, to welcome my husband at night, I'd put a sprig of parsley in it! I used to deck myself out, put the children to bed, and then wait, no matter how tired I was. Yes, God be praised. Like honey and butter we've been, for more than twenty years. Yes, a blessed life!"

I'd hung all my rose clothes away in a corner of the closet. Some I wore when Ihsan wasn't there, or for women's visits, but since our marriage I hadn't bought a single rose garment.

On the third floor of Lafayette I spotted a beautiful rose blouse of silk sateen, trimmed with delicate lace, warming the body of the wax model. I stood motionless before it, as it lay there over the mannequin's extended arms.

"Ihsan," I said. "Buy this for me."

He gazed unbelievingly into my face; then he smiled and bought it. Wearing my broad, rosy blouse, I sat on his knee in the spacious hotel room. I put my arm around his neck, tickled his face with the silk, wrapped him in its rosiness, and he embraced me joyfully. My inner being slept as I gave myself to him in those rosy clothes; and then my closet was filled with the color I love best.

Still gazing into my eyes, Jalal pulled up a chair and sat facing me.

"Rose is my favorite color," I said.

"I know. It's a transparent color. I like it too."

"So does the revolution, with all its concerns, have time to enjoy what's transparent and beautiful?"

He paused, apparently perplexed by my tone, with its mixture of irony and seriousness.

"Conflict doesn't make life stop, Nadia," he said, "or wipe out its beauty. Quite the reverse. It enriches it. A revolutionary doesn't strip himself of life so as to fight; he strives to better it. Besides, conflict isn't some cocoon where liberation grows, then bursts out into a winged butterfly. It's more complex, in its everyday reality, than it seems to outsiders."

He was excited—tossing the ball into my court.

"And in your struggle. Do the great and the small get an equal chance to discover life's beauties?"

His face reddened. He seemed irritated at where I was leading him.

"We come from a nation," he said, "that's fated to be exposed to conspiracies, and attempts at distortion, by people near and far. And because that's our fate, our conflict's bitter and different from other struggles. A lot of what's said about us is aimed at distorting what we do."

Something inside me was growing with his excitement. Don't you know, Jalal, that I know? Didn't Ihsan tell you, Mr. Gonzales, that I heard you with my own ears? Part of your real face is exposed to me now, and I want to be sure of the details that are left.

"Mr. Gonzales!" I said.

"My name's Jalal, Nadia."

"Mr. Jalal Gonzales. All any of you ever talk about is the plots and intrigues facing you. Hasn't that been enough to unite you? To purge you of the disputes and wrongdoing and mistakes we keep hearing about? Isn't all that reason enough for the revolution to punish, and severely too, anyone who makes mistakes, or does wrong, or goes too far?"

Ihsan arrived, laughing. He'd heard my last sentence.

"I don't believe it!" he said. "The moment you arrive, the two of you start discussing great causes! Don't you realize the world has small, trivial things in it, and that they're part of life too? Couldn't you have put the argument off, Nadia, until he'd had a chance to rest? Don't blame her, though, Jalal. The revolution, and its triumphs and mistakes—that's the sole topic of conversation in Barqais. They judge you while they're eating stuffed lambs, they talk about going too far while they're drinking whisky. The prices of their women's jewelry and silk clothes are mixed in with gossip about some man of the revolution who owns a Persian carpet. Haven't I said it a hundred times, Nadia? Just ask one of them, or his son, to leave his job or his business and join the revolution, and see what you get! What they want, deep down inside, is for things to stay the way they are, so they can keep their positions and their projects. Just ask even the most zealous ones and see!"

"We don't want everyone to fight on a single front," Jalal broke in, puzzled by his agitation. "In fact it would be pretty difficult to set one up. In any case, what you said is unfair. A lot of the leaders were living abroad, but they still left everything behind and joined the revolution."

The first swimmer was a girl about eight years old. She was wearing a colored two-piece swimsuit, the top hiding something still undeveloped, for all the designer's insistence on making a woman out of her childish body. She shook her long thick hair, and, as she jumped into the pool, the cold water splashed the tiled edge, together with Jalal's back and my feet. As she raised her head above the water, Jalal waved to her and smiled. She responded with a wide grin, then, seeing our interest, dived under once more. Jalal continued.

"Every revolution, Nadia, past or to come, has its mistakes, because the human mind's weak. But propaganda about our mistakes, and the way they're exaggerated, is part of the conspiracy against us. We don't care what our enemies say. At the start, with no time to choose, we accepted anyone who wanted to join. The revolution, though, acted like a sieve, and a lot of people were sifted off. We've plenty of challenges ahead of us, but our sole concern, no matter what other people say, is our nation's constant faith in us."

"Faith, Jalal Natour, begins with those small things of anything whatever. Faith, Mr. Gonzales, is attaching yourself to the particles and remembering their tiniest details. In Barqais I've come to know what it means, being united with the far-off homeland. When I first arrived, people were talking about it, saying they belonged to it. It was a dream planted in their eyes and hearts—in your estrangement, voluntary or forced, you find out how deeply those particular elements of faith flow in your veins, drawing you to the homeland—you might lack the courage to make a decision, or do what needs to be done, but the bond comes to bind you without your knowledge. It's only when you're far away that you realize how it grips your soul and your mind."

Jalal rose to his feet, and Ihsan did the same.

"We need to clarify many matters, Nadia," Jalal said, as he took his leave. "We'll talk when Ihsan and I come back, after we've finished some business we have in Athens."

The swimmers took to the pool, and I sat alone, brooding about Jalal. What did I want from him? I couldn't define it exactly. Did I want to see his true face? Wasn't what I knew the true him? The swimmers grew noisy, and I fled to my room.

When Ihsan came back, he sat gazing at me. Seeing me sunk in depression, he begged me to go out with them.

"Nadia," he said, "we need to look like a family on its summer holidays. So as to divert attention from him and keep his identity secret."

"I'm fed up with the sea, the mountain and everything else. I don't know why you expect me to stay here. Or when there's going to be an end to all this waiting, when I don't even know what we're waiting for."

He gave a cheerful laugh, trying to pull me from the sofa.

"Come on, get up. Tomorrow it'll all be over. We'll leave the day after tomorrow."

I held back, and he let go of me.

"I want to know what's going to happen tomorrow!"

"I'd tell you if I knew myself. When I do, darling, I'll tell you everything, rest assured. Jalal's the one who arranged the whole thing."

He was lying, and he laughed as he saw I didn't believe him.

"All we need, Nadia," he said, "is your prayers and good wishes."

I switched on the television and watched a Greek tourist program right through. I didn't understand what was being said, but the dance at the end reminded me of the lively steps of Kazantzakís's hero. I put out the light and sat on the terrace. The sea breeze stung me, and I went back into the dark room, where time passed slowly as I waited.

When I heard his key in the door, I pretended to be asleep. He switched on the light, exposing my face, and I made a convincing show of being in a deep slumber. He embraced me, kissed my forehead several times, then, finding no response, left me alone. Muttering, he got ready to sleep. Then he suddenly whispered: "Nadia. Jalal's getting married."

His words stung me, but I resisted my first reaction, striving to stay quiet for all the turmoil deep inside. Wonderment and amazement! Getting married! A sense of mortification welled up from my very heart.

What am I to you, Jalal Natour? Do I sense in you things I created, dreamed of, ever since that illusion of you following me through the alleys of Damascus and being there behind the curtains? Have I invested the robe of reality with a feverish illusion? Because I wanted your love, did I contrive to believe something that never happened? Jalal, getting married! After he held my hands in his soft palms this morning—and the longing was in his eyes—I saw it—I didn't imagine it. So how can it be he's getting married?

Ihsan touched my bare shoulder. I felt sickened.

"Nadia—"

He kissed my forehead, my hair, moved his finger along my lips. I lay there without moving.

"Nadia. Jalal's getting married."

I said nothing.

"To Najwa Thabit."

I said nothing.

"You remember meeting her, when she came to Barqais?"

Najwa Thabit. She'd been carrying that sword studded with gems, but there'd been no gleam in her eyes. She hadn't stretched out her hand to eat a single mouthful from a table piled with cooked lambs and appetizers. The assignments she'd taken on were famous the world over. A courageous girl with a strong personality, no doubt influential within the group.

"Will Najwa Thabit be useful to you in your deals?" I asked.

He gripped my shoulder and shook me angrily.

"They're not our deals," he said, trying to lower his voice. "You know that, Nadia. We're both doing this for the cause! Why won't you believe that? You don't know how important money is. And as for his marriage, it's because he loves Najwa Thabit. She's his comrade."

Yes, he loved her, of course he did! Congratulations!

I pulled the cover over my head, curling up on my side of the bed. Ihsan patted my back. Then I heard his regular breathing, while I remained in turmoil. I decided I had to know.

❧

Ihsan left in a rush, and I couldn't do anything. The noise of the swimmers in the pool was mounting. From the terrace the road to the mountain looked empty. A lone tree could be seen at the top, marking the beginning of a small, thickly set wood.

I was mentally climbing that road, when I heard Jalal loudly waking his brother.

"It's one o'clock, Ihsan. It's only two hours to your appointment. Are you still asleep?"

As I raised my head, my headache seemed lighter. Then it got stronger again from the noise of the water streaming down on Ihsan's body. He was humming cheerfully. As he turned off the shower tap, he called out: "Do you want to come with me, Nadia?"

"Where?"

"To the airport."

"Are you meeting someone?"

"No, just sightseeing."

He didn't seem to be joking.

"With Jalal?"

"Alone."

I refused, and he didn't insist. I sipped my coffee slowly, but he bolted down his breakfast, then went off looking handsome and elegant.

The rays of the sun lit up the mountain in front of me, vanquishing its shadows. The solitary tree seduced me with its loneliness, and I submitted. Behind was the small wood of old pine trees, some way apart, far less thickly set than they'd seemed from the hotel balcony. The path to it had been trodden by many of the hotel guests, whose feet had made a clear path amid the thorns and the dry grass of the previous spring. The scattered houses of Glyfada, the summer resort of the rich, looked poorer and smaller as you moved on to the foot of the mountain.

Wild winds had bent the lone tree's trunk, and, with the passage of years, it had grown crooked, its branches soaring high above, some of them dangling.

I sat against the trunk, seeing mountains and valleys stretched out before my eyes. There were groves of green olive trees here and there, and scattered small houses, at the forks of roads or on mountain slopes. I stayed there until sunset. Then, as the chirping of crickets grew louder on the western side of the forest, and I began to feel lonelier and more depressed, I descended the earth track made by the walkers' feet.

I caught sight of him the moment I entered the hotel lobby, reading his English newspaper and drinking coffee. I ran off. Yes, I ran, without knowing why. I rushed toward the elevator, scared of meeting Jalal alone, and of something else I didn't understand. As he raised his eyes and caught sight of me in his turn, I panicked and sought the safety of my room. I felt incapable of acting naturally.

He came up as I was putting the key in the door.

"Nadia—"

I stood there in the open doorway, not knowing what to do.

"Congratulations," I said.

"On what?"

"Your marriage. To Najwa Thabit."

A smiling light came into his eyes, and I realized how wrong I'd been.

"Nadia," he said, "do we have to go on standing here like this?"

As I closed the door, he sat down in the small salon annexed to the main room and leaned back on the sofa.

"Are you jealous of her, Nadia?" he asked.

It was a direct question, oozing narcissism. He sounded naively rude, somehow adolescent. Not waiting for my reply, he inquired: "Would you have liked to be in her place?"

I was irritated by his silly opening. He seemed to me like an arrogant boy who'd cornered his girl in an alley on a wintry night.

"I've known you were interested in me, ever since we were in Damascus. I could feel the way you cared and still do."

And what about you, Ibn Natour? I thought.

But he didn't give me time to speculate. He got up and moved slowly toward me. I retreated instinctively, seeking protection from the wall.

"I was just a child! And you were the boy next door."

He was in front of me, his arm over my head, pushing me to the wall. There were fumes of alcohol on his breath. I trembled. He was excited now.

"Nadia. You loved me. You still do."

"Can't you understand? Those were the feelings of a child. An adolescent girl."

"You still tremble when we meet."

"But I'm your brother's wife."

Why was I saying that? Why did I let the situation slip from my hand? Why such an idiotic reply, which satisfied his ego and let him usurp what he desired?

"You're his wife because I'm a donkey! I shouldn't have left you to him. I was ignorant too. I was twenty-three, and in your twenties you don't play your own parts—syou play the parts assigned to you by family rules and values, you submit to them, without any power to resist. I was the eldest, and they made me believe my part was to live for them, to make sacrifices, even of the things dearest to me, for the sake of their happiness. I shouldn't have left you to him."

I was shocked. I felt my inner being grow restless, then strike me.

"But I wasn't yours, Jalal."

"Yes, you were."

He added, fiercely: "We should have married one another."

"But I love my husband."

"You're lying. Why are you trembling otherwise? Can you look me in the eye and repeat what you just said?"

His hand crept into my clothes. Feverishly it reached my bare bosom, then his lips roamed over my face and neck. He reeked of alcohol.

"But I'll take you from him. I won't be a donkey for ever."

He tried to pry open my clamped teeth with his tongue. His warm breath and sticky hot saliva hit me, arousing a nausea that made me choke almost. He went on attacking my face, resisting my own resistance—with more and more of that sticky spittle.

A sense of utter loathing welled up inside me. Dreamer though I am, I never imagined an encounter like this, with Jalal, could be so stupid and cheap and sickening. All of a sudden I was just a woman to him. I'd imagined him as panicky on meeting me—beseeching in his confession of love—describing how bitterly he missed me. And now all he could see in me was a female he could throw away or pick up at his leisure. I felt bitter loathing and resentment, and that inner being began to stir, then grow furious, savagely beating my very head.

Where am I in your considerations, Ibn Natour? What does it mean, to leave me to your brother, then come back to take me at your leisure? How could you ever have imagined I'd devote my life to you, to live the life you've planned for me? How do you see me, Jalal? As there awaiting my knight's return? Now I've found the knight's face to be so ugly, and I hate my image in his eyes.

His true face grew still uglier as he came closer. I wanted to tear off his final mask. As his hot lips still inflamed my neck, I said: "How am I to be yours, Jalal?"

"However you like."

"And Najwa Thabit?"

"If you'll agree to be mine, I'll sacrifice anything."

Misunderstanding me, he grew bolder. He started walking me toward the sofa, embracing me fiercely, still reeking of alcohol.

When alcohol storms someone's head, it uncovers the hidden places of the mind, the ones people struggle to conceal and embellish. The threads of feigned tact drop away, along with the chains of hypocrisy in which a person wraps himself before others. He bares his reality, as Jalal's face was bared to me—the face he hadn't allowed us to see before.

I don't know when and how I lifted my palm and slapped him. The giant in my depths was surging furiously out, with boundless strength—my inner being forked in my limbs, turned to a giant liberating itself from the corridors of fear and weakness. I pushed Jalal over the sofa with a strength I never knew I had. I was screaming as my hot tears washed away all that ugliness.

"You're vile! Vile! Do you think I'd spend my whole life waiting for you? That I'd kneel down in front of you when you came back? You're vile and worthless."

I opened the door and stood there.

"Out! Get out of here!"

He was feeling his slapped cheek incredulously, watching my rage in doubt and amazement. Then he left quickly.

I curled up on the sofa, pulled my leg toward my face and covered my eyes with my hand. My desolation wounded me to the heart.

I'm not their woman. Not anyone's woman! I'd always supposed Jalal was what he seemed, that he had real power to touch my inner being, to see it in a sexless way and communicate with it. But to him I'm just a female—and he's a man. I—Nadia al-Faqih—no one will be able to know or possess her. From this moment on I possess myself. They'll see a face unknown to them.

I was still curled up in the room, which had grown dark now, when Ihsan came back. He looked happy.

"Nadia," he said. "What's wrong?"

"Nothing."

"Jalal went off without any warning. He left this note. Didn't he call you, or say anything?"

"No."

He handed me the note. I didn't move for a moment. Then I read it. "Ihsan," it said, "I'll call you later."

"Maybe something important came up."

I said nothing.

"Have you been here like this the whole time?"

"I went to the mountain. I got back a few minutes ago."

"Maybe he tried to call and couldn't get you."

"Maybe."

"Things went just the way we wanted, Nadia. Jalal's a genius. I'm free to tell you now—about his devilishly cunning plan."

He checked his enthusiasm, then went on.

"He does the most wonderful things sometimes! Think of it, Nadia. The plane came in from Eastern Europe and landed there at the airport. The observer was given its papers and exchanged them for other papers he had ready in his drawer. Then he gave one copy to the plane and kept another in his files. It was registered as a plane coming from

Geneva with a cargo of spare parts, and heading for Spain.
The inspectors went on to it, then came out again, without
making any search. Over the next three hours the cargo was
transferred to a Swiss plane standing alongside. We were
watching from the airport tower, drinking tea. Nothing's
impossible, or unbelievable—in fact it's all easier than you'd
ever think. Then the plane took off. For Spain according to
the files, but we knew—the inspector, the filing official and
I—that it was heading for Barqais with spare parts for
planes and cannon. We've done it! If only Jalal were here!"

"I'm tired. I need to sleep."

"I don't feel like sleep. I'm going down to the lounge.
We'll be leaving tomorrow morning."

"Ihsan, this is the last time I'm coming with you on a
business trip. The very last time."

"All right. Although your beautiful face brings me luck."

"I said, I'm not coming."

He went out, slamming the door behind him. I haven't
met Jalal since that day, since I took possession of myself.

FIVE

The Heavenly Bodies Break from Their Spheres

For more than six months you've been waiting for the doors to open, for Nadia to leap up in amazement at what she saw and fling herself gratefully into your arms. You keep brooding, Ihsan, about that look in her eyes. You want to wipe away that confusion between pride and paradise, that sadness too. You brood deeply when you find the time.

Aren't you tired of not understanding her? She's fond of clothes, and perfumes, and jewelry, you have to admit that, but she gets furious when you say things ambiguously, and you have to follow her and explain. It irks and confuses you, too, the way her mood keeps wavering between acceptance and refusal, being feminine and unfeminine. But you haven't time to pursue the matter.

For five months you tried to meet her wishes. Then Jessica Raban called.

"You can come and see it now, Mr. Natour."

There, behind that door, was something lovelier than you'd ever imagined. From the moment the doors were opened, you imagined Nadia filling every corner of this place with beauty and luxury and art. You saw her as a winged butterfly moving from room to room.

But Nadia, as she stood there at the door, said nothing.

The car had swerved its way to the Rue Seize, the splendid residential district of Paris, and stopped in front of a large three-story building. The entrance was grand, but gloomy and narrow too, the way most French entrances are, and Nadia's frown deepened. But when Jessica opened the door of the third floor, and the electric light shone behind the marble statues around the walls of the first room, the space stretched out to three connected halls.

Nadia gazed at the statues. Two were of ancient Greek heroes, in different positions. Then there was a Greek goddess raising her hands in supplication. Another portrayed a slave carrying a big candlestick with lighted candle, fear and apprehension in his face, with one foot off the ground as if running in stone. The classic pieces of furniture, arranged delicately and harmoniously, mirrored the fine taste of its former owner, an international opera singer. The ceiling of the third hall seemed narrower, covered as it was with printed silk cloth, gathered at the center in a loop from which dangled a chandelier with lighted bulbs in the shape of rose-colored lilies. The curtains were of the same cloth, while the walls had many mirrors framed in gilt metal, adding a subtle width to the room. Silk rugs were scattered here and there, matching the furniture with their three colors of blue, rose and gray.

Nadia climbed the two steps up to the dining room. Having no windows, this seemed darkish at first, but it became beautiful the moment Jessica flicked the switch and light spread from the four corners, and from the heavy pure silver candlestick used as a centerpiece.

The nearest wall had on it a traditional painting, showing an outdoor party that had been cheerful ever since the fifteenth century. Women in long, wide-skirted dresses with bare necks and shoulders. Men in formal clothes. One woman, on a swing, was lost in her faraway thoughts, oblivious to the drinking and festivity. On one side the waters of a crystal stream flowed just as they were flowing when the painter pulled away his brush.

The main bedroom was vast, shaded in dominant blue. Facing the splendid bed was a sofa upholstered in blue velvet and framed with gilt wood. Nadia went up to it, sat down, then lifted her legs and stretched full length above it. Leaning on her arm, she seemed a natural part of the surroundings.

"Congratulations, Nadia!"

You took the deed of sale from your inside pocket and handed it to her. She seemed happy as she looked it over.

Was there any need to tell her of the struggle you had to buy it? How you haggled and bargained while the owner, the famous opera singer, debated whether to rid herself of her memories, along with the tycoon who'd rejected her to marry another woman, or whether to hold on to the ghost of her lost love?

"Raise the price as high as you need to, Mademoiselle Raban."

She answered you quietly.

"There are some things, Mr. Natour, you can't buy. People's feelings and memories, for instance."

You accepted her answer without anger. But you begged her to do her best—and she did.

Opening her leather handbag, taking her time, Nadia put in the contract, then got up. She took your arm and, smiling, walked you to the door.

Jessica hurried after you, and Nadia suddenly turned to her.

"Are you tied up tonight, Jessica?" she asked.

"No, Madame."

"Call me Nadia, please. Would you like to have dinner with me?"

Jessica stretched out her hand. Nadia kept the hand in hers for the first time since they'd met. Then, gazing at her in admiration, she said: "You're so different from what I imagined."

"For the better, I hope."

"Just completely different. That's all."

It stung you when Nadia, during dinner, seemed to have forgotten you were there. She listened with obvious passion as Jessica talked about the real estate office, her beloved friend, her school days in Geneva and her job in London. She was clever without ostentation, and Nadia, listening in rapt admiration then bombarding her with questions, gave you no chance to change the subject.

After the bellboy had left, Nadia turned and embraced you tenderly, her face, too, showing a fleeting tenderness that had grown rare in the past months.

"Ihsan," she said, "I want to start a real estate office."

"You?"

"With Jessica Raban."

You couldn't believe your ears. She took no notice of the irony in your voice as you said: "An office like that needs a lot of experience. You've never worked before."

"I'll learn."

"Where? In Barqais?"

"In London."

"Are you out of your mind?"

"I was never as sane as I am now. I'll have my own company. And the apartment you bought for me will be our first offer of sale."

"What?"

"You heard what I said, Ihsan."

"And what about me? The children?"

"We'll live in London—and you'll work in Barqais."

As she still clung to your neck, the idea began, with marvelous swiftness, to sparkle in your mind. The bright side was that, as far as Barqais was concerned, your profits, your family, your possessions would be secure against any shocks, against any future developments or envy.

Her body felt warm next to yours. You said: "Jessica's irreplaceable, really, in my office. But I don't feel I can resist you. Give me time to arrange things."

You gave it a lot of thought later. Did she realize, later on, why you'd gone along with her wish?

Ihsan lifted the receiver with some apprehension. He put on the light alongside him, then slammed the receiver back down angrily as he realized what he'd heard was actually the doorbell. It was one in the morning, and he'd arrived in Barqais, with Nadia, just a few hours before.

It was Afaf standing tearfully at the door, her strange appearance a sign of some disaster. He was shocked at the changes in her. She'd shortened her dress, squeezed her body and bared her neck and part of her bosom. For all her wretchedness, her chestnut-colored hair was carefully combed, but her face was without make-up, her nose swollen from weeping. Her features were rather like his own.

"Ihsan," she said. "Faris has gotten married!"

She staggered, and he caught her in his arms. Then, as her constant weeping turned to wailing, Nadia came to join them.

"Just think! I, Afaf Natour, have to share him with

another wife! Has he forgotten all the things he had to go through until I accepted him? You know who she is? You won't believe it—it's an utter scandal—it's Wafaa, the friend of my daughter Narjis. He's married a mere child! Without any shame! As for her parents—those dogs were obviously after his money."

Her sobbing rose, and she let her tired head drop on his chest.

"Where's Faris now?" Ihsan asked.

"That's why he kept going to Damascus. I thought it was business. I hadn't been able to understand him lately, Ihsan. I did everything to please him—changed the color of my hair, my clothes. I enrolled at a beauty institute and lost weight. I never realized his criticisms meant another marriage. The treacherous dog!"

Ihsan patted her back, then led her inside and sat her down. Nadia, meanwhile, said not a word.

The last time Ihsan had seen her had been three months before, when she came with Faris and read them a poem she was due to recite at a charity bazaar, in aid of children of the revolution's martyrs. A local magazine had published her poem, under the heading of "promising writers," and Ihsan had expressed tactful admiration, though Nadia had made no comment until after they'd left.

"You know, Ihsan," she said, "'promising' is a pretty elastic word. The magazine obviously meant it maliciously. There's no actual acknowledgement of talent. It just satisfies the writer's vanity and leaves editor and critic uncommitted. Writers can keep their 'promise' all their lives, and go on for ever without fulfilling it. But if the writer does succeed, then the magazine gets the credit for announcing a new talent!"

He'd been struck by her insight, but upset, too, at what she was implying.

He asked Afaf again: "Where is Faris?"

"In Damascus. He got married tonight. Tomorrow they're leaving for Europe."

"How did you get to hear of it?"

"From her Syrian sister—al-Hemli's wife. His third, can you believe it? She called me tonight, insisted I go and see her. It seemed an odd thing to ask, but I went. She swore she hadn't known anything beforehand, or she would have told me, or else stopped her sister doing something so foolish. Her mother and Faris, it seems, had agreed on complete secrecy until after the marriage, and that she'd be the one to tell me about it first. They're just husband snatchers! No principles at all! And apart from all that, didn't they even think of his daughter—the bride's friend? And that he's as old as her father? But what do they care, so long as he's rich? That bitch had been planning to get him ever since she visited Narjis to study with her. And I never caught on!"

She burst into another fit of weeping. Then Nadia came and stood in front of her, speaking for the first time.

"Afaf," she said, "do you really love Faris that much?"

The question amazed her more than either of them had expected. She stopped crying and started rubbing her hands together.

"Love him? I don't know—I hope he rots, that's all! I won't have him marry another woman—"

Ihsan left them and went into his office. They fell silent as the numbers he was dialing sounded in the other phone alongside them, their eyes glued to the closed door until he came out again.

"I'll take you home now," he said. "Tomorrow we'll go to Damascus. We'll see Jalal there."

No more than a week later, Faris's marriage in Damascus was the talk of Barqais high society, then the details were passed on to the school playgrounds—how Jalal and Ihsan had gone into the newlyweds' apartment in Damascus and forced Faris to divorce her.

Some women swore Afaf Natour had seized hold of the bride's hair and used it to wipe the floor. According to others, Afaf and the bride's mother had quarreled for more than two hours, so loudly that the whole Khatib quarter, usually so quiet, had heard their shouts, along with language to bring a blush to the boldest faces. What everyone agreed was that Faris had paid his young bride 5,000 lira as compensation, then left for Europe with Afaf instead of the child bride.

Those women in the know in Barqais society also told how the sister's bride, the third wife of al-Hemli al-Kabir, shut herself in her room for three whole days when she heard the news. Then she, in turn, went out to her husband with rumpled hair and red eyes, and he left her and went off to one of his other two wives. She promptly got up, took a bath and scented herself, and awaited the coming night with smiles, but secretly cursing relatives and the problems they brought.

When, two months later, Faris and Afaf returned to Barqais, the salons got busy talking about them. How her dress was so short now it showed her knees, how, with studied casualness, she let it ride when she sat down. How she'd dyed her hair, which looked yellow and carefully fluffed. How her perfume still hung in the air after she'd left. How she spoke with more assurance now, whereas Faris kept quiet in Ihsan's presence, in a way Nadia and the others had never known before.

Once, after they'd gone, she asked: "What did you do to him? You and Jalal?"

He laughed, then shrugged his shoulders.

"Nothing. The fellow came to his senses, that's all. A man turns gray, then marries a child the age of his own daughter? It's a scandal! It wasn't proper for him or us, he saw that for himself. He just needed someone to open his eyes. He backed off on his own account, believe me."

Then, knowing she hadn't believed him, he added: "Faris is a donkey anyway. Maybe we could have forgiven him a fling of some sort, if the news hadn't reached Barqais and affected his marriage. But he's a mule and he'll never be anything else!"

❦

There was a rush among the people on the sidewalks, and some of them hailed taxis as the dark summer clouds thickened, spread, and then covered the London sky with sullen gloom. Then the rain started pouring down. Ihsan, drinking his scalding hot coffee, watched the scene through the window of the café in the Park Tower Hotel overlooking Knightsbridge.

Summer, back there, was engraved on his childhood memory. It was more beautiful too—none of the London rains or the infernal heat of Barqais. Whenever it got hot, his mother would let down the curtains. How well he remembered that far-off house, right down to the last detail. It was all rooted in his mind: those pots on balconies and at entrances, fragrant with every kind of aromatic plant. She'd water them, then rub them, and their smell would spread in his small nose. Would all that ever return?

The return road's hard and long, Ibn Natour, he thought; and before you reach that house, windows and treasures will be opened to you.

For some moments his gaze was riveted on her; then he watched her in bewilderment as she came down the street and stood there in front of him. Tall, with her head held high, braving the cold and rain and spreading a rose-colored umbrella trimmed at the edges with gathered lace. She was wearing tight pants that clung to her lovely, gliding body, and a black velvet jacket that reached to her slim hips, revealing a high-collared rose silk blouse that matched her rosy complexion.

When she'd reached the green pots set in the window, he put some money on the table, left his coffee undrunk and hurried outside, ignoring the blonde waitress who'd become used to his generous tips whenever he visited the café.

He couldn't find her anywhere. He checked the whole row of stores stretching along the sidewalk, but she wasn't in any of them. Only when he reached the second turning did he suddenly realize how oddly he was behaving. What's happened, Ibn Natour? There's something strange, something powerful, urging you to chase after her, and you'll do it a second time if you see her again.

A measure of regret and depression seized him when she didn't re-appear. He walked back. His hair was wet from the rain, but he passed his fingers through it without complaint. It's four in the afternoon, he thought. What would you say to her if you saw her? He brooded for a while, then decided to cross that bridge when he came to it.

Thrusting his hands into his pockets, he started pacing the street, hoping she'd come out of one of the stores when they closed at five. Her image was printed on his mind as he absently watched the people walking. On his way back to the hotel he felt his arm suddenly taken and smelled that special perfume.

"Rashid!"

The man's superb elegance irritated Ihsan.

"Ihsan! What a marvelous coincidence! I was going to call you tomorrow. What about some coffee at the Hilton? Or the Ritz?"

"All right. But let's have it here, at the Park Tower."

He pulled him along, deaf to the man's continuing objections. They crossed the street to the hotel, and, once inside the café, Rashid started grumbling, criticizing the café's cramped atmosphere and making fun of the children who were wolfing sandwiches with their Asian nannies. As for Ihsan, he insisted on sitting by the window, hoping she'd appear out of nowhere. He said to Rashid: "I didn't know you were here. Alone?"

"I'm with him. A private vacation."

"Will you have dinner with me?"

"I don't know what he has planned for tonight. I left him with some of his men. If he lets me, I'll be glad to."

"Why don't you call him now and ask him?"

"Now? No, I can't."

"Why? It's not a summit conference, is it? You know the way his clan talks. Go on, call him."

Rashid, embarrassed by his insistence, went reluctantly off. When he came back, his face was still flushed from what he'd heard.

"Why don't we finish our evening somewhere else, Ihsan? I don't feel comfortable here."

He couldn't hide his deep anxiety, and Ihsan, mischievously, insisted on staying there. They moved between bar and lobby and looked in at the restaurant, but felt no desire for dinner. They talked of business matters in Barqais, then, when it was nearly nine, Ihsan accepted he'd lost her.

"If you like, Rashid," he said, "we'll move on somewhere else."

As they were crossing the lobby, passing by the elevator, Ihsan's heart leaped. The elevator door suddenly opened and out stepped the tall, lithe woman, still holding her umbrella. But, even through his own confusion, he thought he saw Rashid's features relax all at once, though he was too engrossed with the woman to be sure.

The porter bowed, smiling, as he opened the hotel door for them, then hurried on.

"Rashid," Ihsan said, in a daze, "did you ever see such a beautiful woman?"

He rushed outside, and Rashid followed him with a smile. She was standing on the steps, holding her tall body erect as a ballet dancer, the cold wind bringing a flush to her cheeks. Soon a taxi stopped, the porter opened its door and she was gone.

Rashid put an arm around him.

"I didn't think you went in for that sort of thing," he said gaily.

"She's not just a thing. She's a nymph. And now she's gone off to her heaven and vanished."

His serious tone cut off Rashid's laugh in mid air—and all through the evening neither mentioned her. But when Ihsan was alone, he imagined her in his arms, and his heart started pounding wildly. He couldn't think how or where he might see her, and he blamed himself repeatedly for exposing his admiration for her to Rashid.

Tomorrow, he thought, and the day after, and every day, you'll have to wait for her to turn up maybe. Is that love, Ihsan? When you don't even know who she is? And how about Nadia? What's possessing you now is quite different from what you felt when you chose to love and marry her. You'd always supposed you love Nadia and no one else; and now your heart jumps and you burn to see this other woman. Only, you have to find her, and wait for her too. She might come out from anywhere.

He remembered the meeting fixed for the next day. Still, he assured himself, he'd end that by four. The numbers fell and scattered in his mind—he smiled at the thought of the zeroes stretching out—divided them up—scowled at the thought of Jalal's share; then smiled broadly at the thought of his zeroes going beyond those of His Highness.

꿎

It was a little after four when the delegates left his office. One of them had put on his glasses and sent him a smiling wink, looking every inch the seasoned businessman as he picked up the briefcase he'd left unopened through the meeting.

For two hours they'd talked about everything except the practical arrangements. "You'll know the details later on," Ihsan had told them. He gave an ironic smile at the thought of what lay behind those details: dismantled mortar cannons, helicopters and military jeeps would arrive in Barqais under the heading: "frozen meats, agricultural tractors, fishing boats."

In the bathroom attached to his office, he combed his hair carefully, then selected a lotion from the row of bottles before him and scented his shaven face. He looked out of the window. Nelson was still there, gazing down at the crowds. As Ihsan was about to close the door, he heard the phone ring.

"Won't you change your mind, Ihsan?" the voice said.

"Sorry, I've a lot to tie up tonight."

"We could meet now."

"I've an appointment at the Park Tower."

There was a pause.

"Right now?" Rashid asked.

"Yes, right now."

"Some other time then."

Ihsan checked the lobby, then the bar, before heading off to the café. She was sitting near the window, facing the door. Her blue silk dress was so densely reflected in her eyes that they seemed blue as the sea. She had a black band around her hair, which fell in waves on her shoulders, yellow as fields of wheat. When heaven answers wishes, realizes them by a miracle, it makes a person wonder. Has it brought happiness, or rather frustrated the enjoyment of longing and search?

She was sipping her coffee as he reached her table.

"May I sit down?" he asked.

Her eyes wandered over the empty chairs around about her.

"Of course," she answered coolly. "I was just leaving anyway."

He sat down.

"Now?" he remarked. "In all this traffic? You've no chance of a taxi. Or are you staying at the hotel?"

She seemed uninterested in his curiosity. She gazed at him, then said slowly: "No, I'm not staying here."

"But I saw you here yesterday."

She thought for a moment, then smiled.

"Are you following me, Mr. —?"

"Ihsan Natour. A businessman from Barqais."

"Have you been following me, Mr. Natour?"

"Why hide the truth? I've been looking for you since I saw you, yesterday."

What he'd said was clearly nothing new or unexpected to her. Confident in her beauty, she went back to sipping her coffee.

"What is it you want, Mr. Natour?"

"Just an innocent friendship."

"And suppose I don't want this friendship, Mr. Natour. What would you do then?"

"Well, I don't say I'd kill myself. But I'd be wretched and miserable to no purpose, and then I'd write my own elegy."

My, my, Ibn Natour. Poetry! After the way that teacher always yelled when he looked at what you'd scrawled in your composition book. "Read, boy! Read, you donkey, and improve your style!"

He was glad to note, from her face, that she was impressed by what he'd said. She gave a rippling laugh. Her eyes shone with interest.

"You mean you write poetry? I thought you were a businessman."

"A businessman during the day and a poet in love at night. Could I offer you another cup of coffee, Miss—or Mrs.—"

"Mrs. Redenstein. Angela Redenstein. And I prefer tea."

He felt comfortable and relaxed, like someone who's finished a race. He ordered tea for the two of them.

"You're married then, Mrs. Redenstein?"

"Divorced."

A sudden happiness enveloped him as she said the words so simply, without regret.

"How could anyone abandon a woman like you?"

"Divorced, Mr. Natour, doesn't necessarily mean he abandoned me. Why shouldn't I be the one who left him?"

She spoke the words distinctly, her tone that of a teacher correcting an error of fact.

"How about you?" she went on. "Are you married?"

"Yes."

"Children?"

"Three. And you?"

"No children. Thank God."

"Do you live here?"

"Here and in Geneva."

"You work?"

"As an agent for a company selling the finest watches and jewels in the world."

"Your work must give you the chance to meet a lot of people."

"Only the elite—and the rich."

Their eyes met over his gold watch. The light sparkled from the diamonds set around it, and they both laughed.

"How long are you staying here?"

"I'll be leaving the day after tomorrow, at noon."

"Would you accept an invitation to dinner?"

She pursed her lips ironically.

"On condition you'll recite some of your poems to me."

"Or that you sell me some of your products. That would be easier. But could I suggest a bigger deal? That we make a firm effort to get to know one another and become friends?"

"That seems civilized and rational, Mr. Natour."

After a lengthy evening at the Ritz, they reached the place where she lived in King George Street. She shook hands with him at a distance, and his dreams evaporated.

This woman hadn't been easy, even if she had accepted the dinner invitation so easily. He kept her hand between his own and said mischievously:

"Would you show me your products, Angela? I want to buy a watch."

She laughed.

"We don't work after five, Mr. Natour," she said firmly. "And we only receive clients on our business premises."

"May I see you tomorrow? For dinner?"

"All right."

She closed the glass door and waved to him. Then she went into the elevator without turning to look back at him.

⚬⚬⚬

She was still awake when she answered his call.

"Are you trying to tell me, Mr. Natour, that it's love at first sight?"

"More than that even."

"Your rush frightens me. Real feelings don't start in such an unruly way."

"I don't agree at all. We easterners are born with strong, true feelings and they keep burning. We don't try and quench them or put them in ice trays."

As she said nothing, he went on.

"Angela, do you have to work tomorrow? Suppose I buy two watches, and you give me your time. What do you think of that?"

"Mr. Natour," she said firmly, "if you'd really like to see me, we'll meet at five, after I've finished my work."

With that she hung up, without saying goodbye.

Next day, though, she was brighter and more communicative. She was, she told him, descended from German princes in Luxembourg, but her ancestors had given her a good background without the wealth to go with it. She'd studied business administration and married a bourgeois colleague whose father owned an international factory making car tires, along with some stores in London and Paris. Her parents had opposed the marriage, despite his wealth, because he lacked noble background and refined taste.

"But I loved him," she went on. "Or maybe I wanted to rebel against their traditions, so arrogant even though they had no money. But, when we were married, I found money couldn't bridge the gulf between our upbringings. We separated to be surer of our feelings—I went on working with the company and he went to Paris, to work at designing and manufacturing ready-made clothes. We used to send one another cards and letters, and we met two or three times, but the gulf was much wider than we'd ever supposed. So we divorced."

As he said nothing, she added:

"You know, Ihsan, human feelings have only one enemy—time! Even civilized relations come to seem silly as time passes, and you forget them."

That night she won at roulette, while Ihsan lost, and she laughed a good deal. As he stood by her door, she suddenly embraced him and kissed his cheeks. Taken by surprise, he didn't realize what had happened until she'd already walked off.

"Good night," she said.

Why, he thought, did you just stand there like a donkey?

Why did you lose your chance?

She closed the door and walked to the elevator, without looking behind her. He drove back to the hotel.

"Yes, Mr. Natour?"

"Jessica, book me a place for tomorrow on the first plane to Paris. Just one seat. And book a suite at the Plaza Athenée."

When he arrived, the receptionist welcomed him with a bow, but shot him a wary, doubtful glance when he asked: "Is my suite next to Madame Redenstein's room? I'm her fiancé, and I want to give her a surprise. Didn't my secretary tell you when she reserved the suite?"

The receptionist, confused but still wary, checked the ledger.

"I'm sorry, sir. No one told us anything."

"But that's the sole reason I came to your hotel."

"An arrangement like that would appear out of the question, sir. I'm sorry."

Ihsan took out a thousand franc note and placed it carefully in his passport. The man was still watching him. Ihsan extended the passport.

"Do what you can. Haven't you been in love and enjoyed surprises, Monsieur—"

"Jean-Jacques, sir. I'll see—"

He re-checked the ledger for some moments, then shook his head regretfully.

"Impossible, I'm afraid, Monsieur Natour."

Ihsan took out another thousand francs, and put the note alongside the first one. The receptionist smiled.

"What would you say, Monsieur Natour, if we move Madame Redenstein from the second floor to the fifth, next to your suite? That would seem easier."

Silently, Ihsan showered the man with venomous curses. He took out a hundred franc note.

"Will you call me, Jean-Jacques," he said, "when the lady comes to her room?"

"Certainly, Monsieur Natour."

She couldn't believe her eyes when she saw him. She stood rooted to the spot after she'd opened the door. Ihsan hastened to close it, then took her in his arms, with longing, just as he'd dreamed of doing since the moment he first saw her. She clung to him.

"Angela—I couldn't stand it. I had to see you."

She stayed in his suite until morning. After she left, he made a call.

"Nadia, I'm in Paris. I'll be here for three days, and I won't be able to call you during that time. Then I'll be going back to Barqais."

He heard her voice from the other end. There was neither objection nor warmth in it.

"All right. Call me when you can."

❧

"Mr. Rashid's here, Mr. Natour."

This was a surprise. He hesitated, then said: "Send him in. Have some coffee brought right away."

Rashid, though, didn't reach for his coffee. His smile was laconic.

"I've come to ask for your help, Ihsan."

Ihsan sat up straight, placed one palm over the other and listened curiously.

"You know, Ihsan, the oil market's fiercely competitive. Although marketing's no problem for us normally, we're starting to think of markets untapped by other people, ones that are thirsty for oil. You're in touch with these markets, and you could make them available to us through your personal means and connections. As I'm sure you know, our present capacity means we can make long-term contracts, and we're actually looking at a current surplus which we could, if others were agreeable, sell under the carpet. A carpet we'd extend, through you and Jalal, to the same Red markets it would be the devil to get into otherwise. Actually, you're lucky to have a brother like that—if I had one, there'd be no limits to what I could do. But the important thing in all this is to keep His Highness out of the picture. If he found out about it, he'd have no mercy on us, or on his son. And if the Shyoukh came to know, there'd be hell to pay!"

The self-assurance in Rashid's tone made Ihsan utterly furious. How dare Rashid talk as though he were holding the reins?

"Look, Rashid," he said, trying to hide his anger, "I don't like mixing business and I prefer to stay out of all this. And, quite apart from that, I wouldn't do anything behind His Highness's back. Also, Jalal isn't a merchant—he works only for the welfare of his group. You must understand that."

Rashid shook his head ironically.

"Of course," he said, giving certain of his words an insinuating emphasis, "what we're offering isn't much compared with spare parts and fishing boats. But if you consider the proposal more carefully, and how it would work out in the long run, you surely wouldn't want to miss out. You know, don't you, the old Arab saying? 'A little all the time is better than a lot now and again.' Didn't they teach you that at school?"

Ihsan nodded, laughing in spite of himself. But he spoke firmly.

"I'm not doing anything behind the man's back, Rashid. If he gives me instructions to open up the markets for you, then I'll do it on the spot. And if his son, your man, can get his father's consent, again I'll open them, and I won't take any commission. Otherwise I want nothing to do with it."

"What an upright fellow you are! You refuse, before you even know what your commission is?"

"Yes."

"Even if there were two commissions, one from him and the other on the side?"

"Whatever!"

Rashid crossed his legs, leaned back, then, with a casual air, took out a small, elegant envelope.

"Be careful! If you read what's in here, you might be persuaded."

He flung it down on the desk. It fell alongside Ihsan's folded hands. Ihsan didn't move.

"Rashid, I'd advise you to take back your proposal and stop wasting both our times."

Rashid walked toward the door, while Ihsan remained seated. Then, suddenly, Rashid turned around, took out a larger envelope and flung that down on the desk too. It landed beside the first.

"If you don't like the first," he said, "maybe the second will make you think again."

He closed the door, pursued by a muttered, venomous curse from Ihsan.

For some moments Ihsan stared at the envelopes. Then

he lifted the second, opened it and was overtaken by dizziness at the sight of three photos. In the first Angela was clinging to his arm, resting her head on his shoulder and, in her other hand, holding something he'd bought her from a top Paris store. In the second he was embracing Angela in front of her apartment on King George Street. The third had been taken at the Ritz restaurant, when she'd suddenly embraced and kissed him.

How is it that a mind becomes totally void when taken by surprise? He hadn't noticed anything amiss during that dinner at the Ritz. Angela had glowed with happiness as she talked, ate and looked into his eyes shining with love. All day he'd been reflecting on the most suitable moment to surprise her, and he'd decided on this one. He'd handed her the long blue envelope, folded in the middle so as to show only her name, which he'd written in italic script.

She opened it curiously, smiling, then her pupils widened and the blueness shone bewitchingly, in long waves. He waited a little, then took the key from his pocket and gave it to her.

He pulled back in instinctive reaction as she leaned toward him, then submitted as Angela embraced and kissed him.

"Ihsan," she said, "I love your crazy ways."

"You mean our relationship's going to stay secret, Ihsan?"

"I'll announce things as soon as I'm ready."

She hadn't asked him again, not even once, accepting what he did, though he saw the question in her eyes whenever he met her.

"I hope you'll like your new apartment," he said, "and that I'll find there's a place for me there."

"Isn't it enough," she said sadly, "that you live in the owner's heart? Aren't you being a little greedy, Mr. Natour?"

She embraced him once more, and he was happy. Just who'd photographed that moment, and when exactly had it been? The first embrace or the second?

He examined the pictures a number of times, and, for all the disaster at hand, an overwhelming longing for her grew inside him. Then, from this growing yearning, Nadia's face began to appear, definitely special and near. He wondered: do you love Nadia, Ihsan? But you want the two of them equally, one as a wife and the other as a lover. And you can't break away from either, or sacrifice one for the sake of the other.

He picked up the first envelope. On the paper inside, in beautiful English handwriting, was written as follows: "Present production and export... Proposed production and export... Commission: on each barrel: two cents to the son of His Highness, one cent to Rashid, one cent to yourself." Rashid's name and phone number followed.

The numbers chased one another in front of his eyes. Zeroes, Ihsan, he thought, just as many zeroes as the ones you're used to now. The commission's small in itself, but it's on a production of a million barrels a day—like a gently flowing stream that conceals its pitiless depths—and when they flow on, into those closed Red markets, the streamlets will take on strength, move into flood. Everyone around you will drown in wealth.

Faces appeared from the two envelopes to assail his mind. Nadia—His Highness—the children—Faris—many others. This Rashid's taken you by the throat, he thought, ready to use the choking as best he can. You have to seek Jalal's help. Even if you had to share the cent with him, there'd still be plenty of zeroes, going on day after day.

Resting his head on his hands, Ihsan sat there brooding until darkness engulfed the office. Then he put on the light and dialed the number.

"Rashid. I'll see you tomorrow morning in my office."

༺༅༾

"We have to find him, Mrs. Natour. It's imperative."

"I've told you, Mr. Black, I don't know where to find him. He hasn't called me since he left."

"This is a disaster. We'll have to act today, or tomorrow at the very latest, before the news spreads."

"What can we do?"

"We'll have to sell."

"Well then, sell."

"I can't take sole responsibility, Mrs. Natour."

"Then sell, I tell you! I'll take full responsibility."

Silence.

"Did you hear me, Mr. Black?"

"I'll need a written authorization, Mrs. Natour."

"Put it in the form you want, then send it for me to sign."

Ihsan couldn't believe what I'd done. He just gazed at us silently, as Mr. Black explained to him how I'd acted wisely, saved our share price by selling, in one transaction, all our shares—his, our children's and mine—for a hundred pounds a share, before, just a week later, the price fell to ten pounds. We owned twenty percent of this textile company's shares, and Mr. Black had come to tell me how he knew for certain, from inside information, that the president of the board was about to be investigated over some foul play in the accounting, and that unrest among the work force was growing into open revolt, that they were getting ready for a long strike. If that happened, the factory would stop production for months maybe, because a large part of the equipment would need renewal and maintenance and the workers were demanding better conditions. The fraud within the management had lowered morale among many in the work force, and, as a result, quality and quantity alike had suffered within a cruelly competitive market. If the news were to spread beyond the factory, the market would slide as small shareholders sold; and, if the board failed to resolve the strike, it would lose face for a long time to come. That's why we had to sell our shares immediately, while the price was still high, rather than wait for others to sell at a low price. If, later, we sensed a potential improvement, we could buy back what we'd sold at the bottom of the market and wait for the price to soar again.

I was convinced by what Mr. Black said. And, not knowing how to find Ihsan, I'd acted on my own initiative, saving three million pounds, our stake in the factory, from otherwise certain loss.

Ihsan checked the figures and order of sale.

"When I'm away, Mr. Black," he said finally, "refer in the future to Mrs. Natour."

That didn't make me happy. I was in the grip of a strange feeling. I realized at that moment how distant Ihsan had become, even when he was with me. He was drawing further and further away, and I hadn't the time to understand or act. Ever since my inner, rebellious being had burst out, I'd been running, panting, along tracks and side tracks, seeking a self I'd wanted, dreamed of, shaped. Ihsan too was preoccupied with something I'd bypassed, something he was hiding from me. I'd stopped listening even to his simple observations.

"Ihsan," I said, "I've registered at the American College, here in London. I want to study business administration."

His face went pale with anger.

"Without telling me? You think I can agree to that?"

I replied calmly, so as to keep a rein on the situation.

"How am I supposed to keep you informed on new developments in our lives, when you don't even tell me where you are and what you're doing? You just disappear without trace! Tell me where you're going to be, and I'll ask your opinion before I decide something."

He ended the dispute as suddenly as he'd started it, and I felt profoundly depressed. His indifference toward what I did meant I could no longer enjoy capricious freedom. I wished he'd made some objection instead, that he'd stormed or raged.

So, Ihsan ended the dispute, and I started studying. Now each of us was preoccupied with something the other didn't understand and held back from asking about. Ihsan pulled at the bed cover, turning his back.

"Do as you like, if that's what you want."

"But I want you to make a donation."

"Who's it for this time?"

"For Zahrat al–Mada'in.[13] Why are you laughing?"

"No reason."

You were astounded, Ibn Natour, by that word "advertisement" under the information, before you even read the seven lines under the picture. There was Nadia amid a group of women wearing folk costume, smiling happily, extremely elegant, the big diamond adorning her neck. She must have forgotten to take it off. And there beside her stood the president of the Arab Women's Association here in London.

"Your wife's someone special," Angela had commented.

"How can you tell just from a picture?"

"But I've seen her."

This gave you a jolt. Angela laughed.

"Don't be frightened. I didn't say: 'Mrs. Natour, I'm your husband's mistress!'"

"All right, all right. Where did you see her?"

"In her office. I asked her to buy me an apartment, on a fictional pretext. And would you believe it, she and her partner found just what I asked for. I had to back out, before I got in deeper."

Nadia wouldn't let go. She nudged him again.

"Ihsan, are you going to make a donation?"

"How much do you want?"

"I want you to bid for something in the charity auction. A model of the Dome of the Rock, made from shells."

"Just as you like."

She leaned over and kissed him.

"Do you know what they say about you over there? Our president was there last week, and when she mentioned your name, they said: 'A lot of families are supported by the money Ihsan Natour gives.' And they told her about your donations for Jerusalem, the foster mother organization,[14] the research foundation. Just think! She was telling me things about you I didn't know myself."

He paused, then said: "I always receive letters of thanks from headquarters."

"What would you say, Ihsan, to a 10,000 pound donation from my office for the study institute? It needs support for its cultural and national activities. Is that enough? You know, we've added this year's profits to the capital. Is it enough?"

"Do what you want."

"And how about you? Don't you want anything at all?"

She came closer to him, but he didn't move. This woman, he thought, who rushes and collects illusions, what does she want from you, and from herself? She's certainly changed. She wears silk and weeps for the distant homeland, at one and the same time! But when she plunges into some work she really cares about, she becomes more delicate and sensitive—and, for all her changeable moods, you love her just as you love the other one.

What fool was it said you can't love two at the same time? You do, Ihsan, and that's why you're so wretched, why you don't even know which one you'd sacrifice if you had to. Do you have to fling them both into some raging sea, so as to know which one you'd save first? Then find you're on the shore and love them both? Your only course is to keep Nadia free and occupied, so she won't be able to find out about the mistress. Aren't you, when all's said and done, happy with what she does—and with what you do? The others are happy enough too. Don't they talk about how you're supporting so many families? Didn't you plan for this, and succeed? And when Jalal, in that first deal, gave you a check for 20,000 pounds, he asked you to write another for the same amount and send both checks, in your name, to one of the revolution's foundations. You'd send those amounts, large and small, and get back letters of thanks and appreciation, without anyone ever asking, or caring, how you came by your money. Jalal, along with a friend of his, put his money in a chain of restaurants in Cairo, and you invested in the Forum Hotel in London.

෨෧෨

When Abdulrahman al-Hemli asked him to dinner at the Ritz, Ihsan agreed at once. Their connection went back to the time before His Highness had come barging in and ordered al-Hemli to transfer Ihsan's warranty to him—so that Ihsan had started working with His Highness, who'd opened the doors of wealth to him. Al-Hemli had been an agreeable man to work with, and, after Ihsan left him, they'd made a point of exchanging cards and gifts on various occasions. And when Ihsan moved to London, al-Hemli's name stayed on the list of official cards the secretary would send out at the two annual feasts.

Abdulrahman al-Hemli rose to his feet the moment he saw the waiter conducting Ihsan toward them. With him was a young man about thirty years old, with a neat mustache, and a skillfully trimmed beard covering his pointed chin, adding a touch of roundness to his long face. He had wide eyes and a fine nose.

"This is Hamed al-Ghamry," al-Hemli said. "First Secretary at the Barqaisi Embassy in Paris."

The young man smiled. His white teeth gleamed, complementing the sparkle in his black eyes, which were edged by long curly lashes. When he shook hands with Ihsan, his grasp remained limp.

Al-Hemli got straight down to business, as he'd always done when discussing deals. He spoke clearly and to the point. Having ordered dinner, he said briskly: "Hamed al-Ghamry's been attached to our embassy for two years. He's an Oxford graduate, he's registered for advanced studies, and he's achieved what a lot of others have failed to do. No surprise in that. He's a chip off the old block!"

Al-Ghamry, the minister. Ihsan had seen him a number of times, before and after he became a minister in the first cabinet formed in Barqais following independence. The Shyoukh had picked out a number of tribal heads and allotted them the various ministries. Al-Ghamry had been given the Ministry of Economics and Commerce, for he was, in the first place, the Shyoukh's uncle and had been responsible for distributing food rations during former droughts in Barqais, winning the respect of the people, who praised his sense of justice. He'd had a shrewd, perceptive mind, and the Shyoukh had always sought his opinion when a company presented a work scheme for Barqais. This al-Ghamry had founded his companies after he'd met the young Abdulrahman al-Hemli and noted his ambition and perspicacity. Thereafter he'd devoted his time to his horses and camels, nursing them through sickness and sorting out their blood lines, and once a year he'd invite the Shyoukh and the men of Barqais to dinner, ending this with a camel race. Al-Hemli and al-Ghamry had been sole agents for the biggest and best companies in Barqais, before the Shyoukh finally took matters into their own hands and distributed them fairly among the others. Al-Ghamry's fortune had been enormous, and the Shyoukh had believed, on the basis of this, that he was the fittest person for the Ministry of Economics and Commerce, where he'd presided until his sudden death. He'd been taking a siesta on his ranch; and, when the servants eventually grew anxious at how long he'd been asleep, they found his body was already cold.

"Hamed al-Ghamry," al-Hemli said, "has opened a door for Barqais that used to be closed. He's brought about what might be considered a fundamental transformation in the relations between Barqais and France."

They both looked at the young man, who wiped his mouth with his napkin, then put it to one side. When he spoke, it was obvious he'd learned the French accent, though he hadn't yet fully mastered the language itself. He took out a long, thin pamphlet, spread it out in front of them and started talking, pointing to the pamphlet by way of illustration.

"After two strenuous years of cultivating contacts, I've been able to get initial consent to a signed agreement for a four-year contract between France and Barqais, during which time we'll receive two supporting ships, logistical model, each weighing 17,000 tons. Moreover, our military helicopters will be equipped with air-to-land missiles, AC 15. We'll also receive two Dauphin submarines. And, according to the contract, the Thompson Company, electronic specialists, will undertake the construction of a radar system, to include alarm, observation and follow-up stations, contact centers and a marine operation management for defending the Barqaisi coasts."

He spoke with confident knowledge, and the figures involved started whirling around in Ihsan's head. Other people are working away, he thought, and you're numbed and lost in Angela Redenstein's arms.

"A still more important element in the deal, Mr. Natour," al-Ghamry went on, "is the training of Barqaisi crews to use this equipment. In addition, the company will provide all the services required for support and maintenance. For two years now I've been through talks and attempts, sometimes interrupted, sometimes exhausting, until I managed to get initial consent through high functionaries at the Ministry of Defense, most of whom had had close relations with my father."

"May he be in Paradise," al-Hemli murmured.

"God rest his soul," Ihsan added.

"It was my father's acquaintances who overcame the obstacles. There are still many points subject to negotiation, but they've promised to do their best for me. They knew my father's generosity well enough."

"What price are they asking?"

"Three and a half billion dollars, to be paid in two installments."

Others cook up stupendous deals, Ihsan, while you sleep. You've lost yourself running after women. But Angela isn't like other women. She's a nymph when she's in your arms.

Ihsan feigned indifference.

"How can I help?" he asked.

"Actually, Ihsan," Abdulrahman corrected, "the whole matter rests with you."

"The decision rests with His Highness. Ever since independence he's been the Shyoukh's consultant in security and defense matters. He's the only one who can persuade the Shyoukh to clinch the deal."

"Mr. Natour," al-Ghamry said, "everyone in Barqais knows you're the key to what they buy. If you can persuade him, the deal will go through with no problem. Besides, it was Uncle Abdulrahman's advice to come to you, rather than going direct to His Highness."

"How about your commission?"

"Five percent if we take care of our men in the Ministry of Defense and the Thompson company. Three percent if you take care of them."

"You must realize this has come totally out of the blue. I'll give you an answer in a month."

"Let's make it three weeks," al-Ghamry said.

All was quiet in front of the Ritz as Ihsan emerged into the cold of London. The two men had escorted him to the hotel lobby, and al-Hemli had insisted on embracing and kissing him.

"Don't keep us waiting too long, Ihsan," he said. "The

whole thing's nearly settled."

"Let's hope for the best, God willing."

It was eight hours before the plane for Barqais was due to leave, and he had plenty of time to pack and reach the airport.

⌘

"The incense, Abdullah!"

His Highness called, and the servant leaped lightly up to fetch the censer. Soon the place was filled with fragrance, and the visitors departed one after the other, until they were completely alone. The man's eyes were gleaming with satisfaction, and he started tapping the floor with his cane, as he commonly did when reflecting or when he felt happy.

"You know, Your Highness," the other man said, "that ever since independence all eyes have been turned to Barqais and the places around it, given that you and your neighbors are planning to settle the frontiers. The small matters pending between you attract the attention of merchants, not only outside Barqais but among those residing here and among her native sons. It has come to my knowledge that certain persons have been making important, unofficial contacts abroad, attempting to give the impression they have authority to negotiate and buy in the name of Barqais."

His Highness stopped toying with his cane. He leaned his hands and his chin on it, listening with interest.

"It's come to my knowledge, sir, that officials attached to Barqaisi embassies are attempting, in an illegal and unacceptable way, to exploit their posts by pushing through certain deals. You know the difficulty in tracing sources,

Your Highness! In fact the matter in question needs official ratification if it is to go through. There are others who insist on dealing at a high official level, not with petty pirate outfits like these. The attitudes and actions of these minor officials in our embassies are liable to affect the image of Barqais in other people's eyes, especially if any of them should succeed in clinching even one small deal. It would also encourage greedy people to look for unofficial ways of making deals."

"What's been going on, Ihsan? Who are these officials?"

"Minor functionaries at the Paris embassy. What they've been doing is nothing so very important."

"Have they got anywhere?"

"Was there ever the least chance they would? Even we, acting quite openly, have great difficulty reaching such agreements. How could they succeed? And would a government like the French be persuaded to deal with the likes of them? We've failed with France up to now."

"What needs to be done?"

"The point is, Your Highness, our group and I are already in contact with the French, with a view to making a highly advantageous deal. I don't want stupid interference from petty officials greedy for a commission, who sully our image in front of others. Negotiations are under way, and they're promising, but I need your backing for what we're doing. You're the only one able to provide it."

"Very well. What needs to be done?"

"I'd need a mandate from the Shyoukh to represent Barqais in negotiating the agreements, in the name of the government. The signing and implementation would go through the Shyoukh and the government solely. The mandate would enable me to decide on the size of the deals with the sources I'd meet and the friends who are going to smooth our path. Then I'd come back to you with recommendations for the agreement and final ratification."

Ihsan had prepared his speech with care; for, if His Highness knew what al-Ghamry had actually achieved, he'd never trust Ihsan again. He spread the pamphlet in front of His Highness, just as al-Ghamry had done, and said: "This, sir, is an enormous deal for Barqais; and I assure you the French government is on the point of agreeing. I have this from our friends in the government, who, in the face of certain hazards, are prepared to make a considerable effort to see the matter through."

The man's eyes gleamed admiringly as he listened to Ihsan's explanations, taking note of the smallest details about the helicopters and the Dauphin submarines equipped with missiles. He was entranced by the effectiveness of the radar system proposed by the Thompson Company. As Ihsan fell silent, he asked, suddenly: "When did you arrive, Ihsan?"

"A few hours ago."

"Very well. Go back to London on the first plane and wait for things to develop as we hope."

Ihsan waited in the hotel room. At two in the morning the receptionist called.

"Mr. Jalal is on the line," the sleepy voice said. "I'm sorry to have taken so long connecting you."

"Jalal, I'll be arriving in Beirut tomorrow night. I need to meet your chief on an important matter."

"The chief? In person?"

"Yes. For something crucially important."

"Can I know what it's about? It would make it easier, given the way things are."

"No, I'm sorry, Jalal. It's confidential, between him and me. Please tell them that."

"I'll meet you at the airport."

The moment Ihsan saw him with his guards he realized how much Jalal had suffered from recent ordeals. Suddenly, Jalal said: "I'm tired, Ihsan. I'm thinking of leaving the group."

He'd lost a good deal of weight. His eyes had bags beneath them and were half-ringed with black through lack of sleep.

The car drew off, and they said nothing more in view of the four accompanying guards. They passed the wall of the American University, then the car swerved into Bliss Street and came to a halt at the end. The young guard there stood to attention when he saw Jalal, who briefly returned his salute.

Jalal's apartment seemed modest to Ihsan, given the former's wealth. Your brother, he thought, knows how to play his part. The guard put down the suitcase and went out, whereupon Jalal said, by way of explanation: "We got divorced last week."

"Couldn't you have made up somehow?"

"The differences were ideological, Ihsan, not about small things. Feelings can't change an ideology. It isn't subject to bargaining. Separation was the only course."

Ihsan stifled a laugh, as he pictured ideologies as some entity sharing their bed. Curse you, Ihsan, he told himself, for letting a thought like that cross your mind!

"I couldn't go on any longer, Ihsan, not even with the group. Most likely I'll be leaving them soon anyway, but first I have to straighten out and clarify certain matters. I don't want to tangle with them. Their notion of conflict's different. They have a lot of problems with others, and they're in difficult circumstances. It's all too much."

"How about the others? How do they keep going?"

"It's not in my nature to tolerate mistakes and ignore them. You've known me since we were children together. Here you could disagree with others, because some people take orders blindly. The problem with me is, I always use my head—I can't stop thinking even for a moment."

His anger grew as the words rushed out. Ihsan's lips parted in a pale smile, like the one on the Mona Lisa, which Nadia insisted was the most wonderful, beautiful smile ever—though he'd been able to see nothing in it.

Jalal poured him a glass of whisky, adding the ice cubes with a jerky motion.

"As you rise to a higher rank in the organization, you take on more responsibility, come closer to the level where decisions are made. That's at the root of our disagreements. A lot of decisions are being taken on the spur of the moment, others are hampered by bureaucracy, as though we were government offices. Then there's the favoritism—the cliques—the wrong actions—things I can't keep quiet about. Believe me, Ihsan, the people lower down are much better off—they fight on the fronts, they carry out the orders they're given. But before an order's given, you have to face the difficulties, the disagreements, the petty struggles. That's why I'm fed up. Financial problems, the hardships of reaching the country, disputes with the Arab regimes—to say nothing of all this bureaucracy, as if we were one of the regimes ourselves. I'm tired out."

He drained his glass in a single gulp. His hand was shaking.

"Do you think, Jalal, you actually can leave without making problems for yourself?"

"I'm not going to dissent from them, or form a group of

my own, or join someone else. I'm leaving the whole works to them. That's going to be my way of protesting, after I've finally talked myself hoarse. I won't cut my ties with them, of course, but I'll deal with them in my own way. I'll support them as much as I can, but without commitment. I don't have to abide by their mistakes or adopt their attitudes in every detail. I'll pick out what I'm convinced by. And where that's the case, I won't grudge them anything."

He poured himself a second drink, then added: "I'm certainly expecting trouble from Najwa Thabit—especially as, ever since the divorce, she's started outbidding me in unswerving loyalty. I swear, Ihsan, a woman's always a woman, even those who work with us. It's the upbringing of generations, complexes piled up along the passage of time. You can't change that so easily, no matter what ideologies or causes lie behind. The human mind's a terrible thing—you can't transform it by controlling it, not beyond a certain point. That's the problem —the female complex is still controlling Najwa Thabit. Everybody knows she has special standing with the chief, especially after the heroic operations she's taken on. Even the chief's started believing what she's been saying about me. I want to get out before things get worse. I'm afraid the others would exploit it. I was feeling as low as I could feel when I called you last week. I'm worn out, Ihsan!"

For many years, Ihsan thought, you haven't felt this kindness and compassion toward him. There's a thick cloud of emotion veiling the distance between you. Why don't you rush and engulf him with this present feeling of yours? Why do you hesitate, now, to tell him you love him? The face of that frightened child on the summit comes back to you. You shrieked as you tripped and wounded your knee.

He came back to you with his love, but you tripped him in your turn, then started racing him to the peak, while he stood there, torn between pity and puzzlement at your shrewdness, then rained children's curses down on you. His face today is a child's face, pleading for help, while you're at your summit and your hand urges you to extend that help—to embrace him and save him.

Sitting there motionless, Ihsan asked: "When do I get to see your chief?"

"We'll have their answer tomorrow morning. Won't you tell me what it's about?"

"Not now. After I meet him maybe."

Jalal was still speculating when, just before dawn, they went to bed.

At the airport Jalal embraced his brother several times and kissed his cheeks. Ihsan struggled to hold back his tears. He thought: You like the apprehension and sense of defeat in his eyes. You loved him, Ihsan, from your childhood on. But he was always stronger than you—better at everything, loved by other people, and that banished your loving feelings. Now, as he wishes you goodbye, with his eyes full of tears, the distance of childhood years has vanished.

"It's all settled with them, Jalal."

"How can I ever thank you?"

They embraced again.

Before he went off to nowhere, Jalal Natour left everything in his apartment for his guards. The low-ranking comrades declared that when his brother, the millionaire, visited their fortress, he gave everyone he chanced to meet a good sum of money. Some of them exaggerated the amounts. "Man," they said, "Ibn Natour supports so many families!" But none of the high-ranking comrades could know just what passed between Ihsan and the chief, who'd shown them the check Ihsan had signed to the tune of half a million dollars. The chief had shaken his head regretfully.

"Poor Jalal," he'd said. "Just think, even I knew nothing of the truth. He never told me he was sick. He used to work with such enthusiasm. Our nation's alive! No day passes without our hearing of this act of heroism, that sacrifice. Our nation has real men! We've lost Jalal, it's true, as a guiding mind; it's tragic about his health. But in any case, working with his brother, he'll support us financially. Such a tragedy—I had no idea he was sick."

His face revealed a pity that moved like a wave to the comrades surrounding him.

Ihsan didn't have to wait long. A week later the Barqaisi ambassador received him warmly in his office. The fragrant incense reminded Ihsan of His Highness's gatherings, and this awoke a sense of friendly gratitude.

The ambassador's face looked different without his national dress, and his body seemed fuller. They sat close together on the comfortable sofa.

"Mr. Ihsan," the ambassador said cordially, "the whole embassy will be at your disposal as and when you wish. We'll arrange any appointments you ask for."

Ihsan opened the official envelope, and the letters danced before his eyes. His Highness had been precise and explicit—the mandate specifically nominated Ihsan to represent the government of Barqais in negotiating the prices and sizes for primary deals, the final decision and signature to rest with the head of state.

When Ihsan left, the ambassador shook his hand firmly.

"I'll see to the matter," he said, "through our ambassador in Paris."

Possession of that mandate left Ihsan feeling somewhat insecure—he'd come out now from under Jalal's protection, to pass through wide gates that would be effortlessly opened to him. The roads, it was true, would be shorter and safer now, but he'd have to face everything alone. Unexpectedly, a sense of confidence, and of his own worth, swept through him.

"Could you step into my office, please, Mr. Black?"

Mr. Black carried out his instructions. Four private bodyguards were hired, four elegant, handsome young men, expert at defending him and themselves. Two of them started following him closely, while the other couple guarded Nadia and the children. She'd grumbled at first, but was convinced when Ihsan explained to her the dangers of being wealthy and a maker of major deals.

Her face expressionless, she handed Ihsan an Arabic magazine published in Paris. She pointed to a column with the title "Pin-Pricks," and he read as follows: "A fighter was recently divorced from her high-up comrade. It remains unclear whether the causes were ideological or mundane. Certain close friends assert the reasons were of a kind liable to irk even a woman busy fighting in the field. Others believe the battlefield was too narrow to hold the two of them, and that he packed his case and left the fortress to her alone. Or perhaps he grew tired of fighting women, preferring to look for an ordinary one.

"Let it be whispered: His brother, the millionaire, paid the comrades half a million dollars as the price of his brother's release."

He read with smiling satisfaction what others had let out about his help for Jalal.

"Is this true, Ihsan?" Nadia asked.

His smile broadened.

"You know what journalists are."

"How about his struggle?"

"He did it for the struggle—to preserve unity after the gulf had widened between him and his comrades. He preferred to withdraw rather than disrupt things."

"And the principles he kept talking about for years? And wanted us to believe in?"

"Principles don't change, Nadia, you know that. But struggle takes different forms."

"Yes, of course. The rich struggle differently from other people. What I do know is that a conflict never varies."

Her bitterness made him uncomfortable.

"What do you mean?" he said, knitting his brow and wondering if she still, even now, cared for Jalal.

"It's clear enough. The rich are shaded by canopies of money, canopies that protect them from the smallest ray of sun. But the poor struggle out in the open, facing danger and anything else that might come."

"Sometimes you talk the way ignorant women do. They can't face danger just like that, without a roof for protection. There are people who do the planning— politically and educationally, through information and finance. Gaining support in these fields is struggle too. It needs abilities as important as fighting ones."

"There's nothing to equal real fighting. Or have you forgotten that, Ihsan? Still, a person looking for justification can always find some way of convincing himself. Is the one who stands in the firing line equal to the one who just sits at his desk or donates money?"

"That's enough now, Nadia. All great causes need both, the front lines and those in the rear. Each supports and protects the other."

"And where is he now?"

"In Greece. He'll work in private business, and he'll be able to support them with money as he promised. That's better for both sides."

Nadia never referred to Jalal again.

꒰ꕥ꒱

From the moment the black official car arrived to escort him from the Plaza Athenée hotel, the atmosphere became charged with the awe of secrecy. His bodyguards stayed in the hotel lobby, and he went with the reserved but pleasant driver. The man remained silent until they'd reached the Ministry of Defense, where he bowed once more and opened the door for Ihsan, who was greeted by a high-ranking officer.

The French never get tired, Ihsan thought to himself six hours later, as he followed the same officer back down the long ministry corridors. And Hamed al-Ghamry had been dead right: these people knew what they were doing. They'd invited him to a business lunch during which he'd watched films of submarines destroying ships, a plane being hit, helicopters flying to and from narrow passes and mountain peaks, ships moving and racing through the ocean waters.

The generals had supplied a non-stop explanation, deluging him with the minutest details. Then the minister had elaborated, pointing out the characteristics and hazards of the deal and the dimensions of the agreement. You only care about one dimension, Ibn Natour, he thought to himself—what you'll be getting at the end of it!

And, for all the minister had said about the hazards and obstacles, Muawiya's hair,[15] he felt, was still between them. The teacher kept explaining to you that story of Muawiya's single hair, which he would never let be cut. These bastards knew all about that before Muawiya ever did! They'd hang you from it with their courtesy, then they'd pull the rug from under your feet, leaving you no idea where you were going to land.

During the second day's meeting the minister came to the point, without for a moment abandoning his cordial manner.

"Monsieur Natour, as a means of establishing privileged relations between France and Barqais, with the specific aim of developing Barqais's wealth and utilizing our country's particular scientific skills, we suggest the construction of a petrochemical plant with French capital. We'd invest for ten years in return for thirty percent of Barqais's revenue from the plant. After five years your government would be half owners of the plant, after a further five years it would be sole owner, the plant to remain strictly under our management during that time. We'd also train Barqaisi cadres to take over the management when the contract expired. Acceptance of this crucial financial project would, for us, greatly facilitate the closing of the agreement you're requesting. It would be the largest agreement signed by our government with any country in your region up to the present time. You are, needless to say, well aware of the hazards surrounding the exportation of weapons of this kind, plus the problems of balance maintenance."

Ihsan lit a cigarette and crossed his legs.

"You must be equally aware, sir," he said, "that there's no point in tying the project to the agreement. The project you suggest is doubtless crucial, but the Barqaisi government could undertake nothing before studying the economic benefits involved."

My, my, Ihsan, he thought, where did you learn all that? Nobody's ever before studied the economic benefit from any projects for Barqais. It's a virgin land, thirsty for any new water! And this project's going to go through, because the French are set on it and they'll link it with whatever they want to. But you have to maneuver.

He didn't miss the minister's ironic smile.

"Naturally, Monsieur Natour, we've carried out a preliminary study and found that the economic benefits for Barqais will, in the long term, greatly exceed those for ourselves."

"There's the question of provisional consent to the agreement. As such, it shouldn't be tied to the project."

"Our government, Monsieur Natour, sees them as bound up together."

Ihsan straightened. Both were ready to pounce.

"That makes it difficult for me."

"It remains one of our conditions."

"In that case, negotiations would be lengthy indeed! You must be aware we can't possibly link the process of defense development in Barqais, planning its frontiers and building up an armed force to protect its coasts, with a financial project that could be executed smoothly at any time."

"In that case, we would, I assure you, be content with simple provisional consent from your government, the details to be discussed later."

They both fell silent. The minister smiled.

"Monsieur Natour, we fully appreciate the efforts of friends in our projects. Here is the first study for the project—you may present it to your government."

Things weren't easy, though. When he accompanied His Highness to meet the Shyoukh, Ihsan realized he was up against an extremely shrewd and perceptive man. His face, seen close up, was younger and more handsome than it seemed in official photographs or on television, where he always assumed a reserved and lofty air.

The Shyoukh listened with the closest interest. Then he began talking, drumming his thigh and gazing steadily at Ihsan.

"The French, the Americans and the British," he said, "are all pimps. They never give without taking something. Industrial development is very much a concern of ours; indeed, I've been planning for it long since, without waiting for the French or any other nation to bring it to my attention."

Abruptly he controlled his anger.

"Tell them, in any case, that I'll study the situation and give them our answer."

Ihsan had to wait just two months, after which Barqais signed the agreement in the French Ministry of Defense. His Highness, accompanied by two military experts, supplied the official signature.

Meanwhile, at the economics ministry, an agreement was initialed between France and the Barqaisi government for the establishment of a petrochemical plant. This was signed on behalf of Barqais by the Minister of Economics and the Shyoukh's consultant on economic affairs.

When Ihsan went with His Highness to see him off at the airport, he had the feeling of someone who'd been running long and slowly in an enclosed space, before speeding up and feeling the distance shorten in front of him, amid the watchful, fearful eyes of those trying to race him, waiting for him to tumble so they could win instead.

He gave the French Ministry of Defense the number of his secret account at the Crédit Suisse bank in Zurich. Then a powerful longing for Angela swept through him, a need to comfort himself with her.

When he met her, his thirst for security was quenched completely. This woman, he thought, sophisticated though she is, makes you feel you're a proper man. She treats you, assesses you, in the light of what you've achieved. You're pleased she isn't concerned with what you were before— whereas with Nadia you feel you're being stripped naked. It irks you the way she knows everything, and keeps it to herself. And yet you love her.

The villa Les Eucalyptus, which he'd bought in Marbella, was too narrow to hold his happiness with her. He'd decided to buy the villa the moment he set foot in its garden and walked down the stony tracks to look it over. He was filled with the feeling that something ties a person to a place at the first glance—something akin to love at first sight. Who said it only happens between people? Sometimes, too, it happens as stones and nature strike you with that bewitching effect.

That was how Ihsan had felt since seeing that blue seat overlooking the trim garden with the lofty palm trees around it, a green lawn with beds filled with roses and fragrant plants. Along the sides of the path were rows of cactus shrubs, stunted or gigantic, reflecting the owner's love of exotic desert plants. Ihsan imagined himself there on the seat, and Nadia's fragrant perfume filled his senses,

engulfing him in longing. Then, as he climbed the spiral
stairs to the upper floor where the bedrooms were, he
pictured himself carrying Angela in his arms. He felt desire
stirring for her too, and so he surrendered to them both,
feeling a double sense of numbness settling within him.
Ihsan had bought the villa, and spent a week there with
Angela, before showing it to Nadia.

ᵕᜨᜩᜭ

The moment he saw the *fedewi* there with another guard,
waiting by the steps of the plane, he realized something was
seriously amiss. The stinging desert cold struck him. Some
of the Arab and Asian airport employees were crowding
around the black car, waiting curiously for a sight of the
important visitor.

The street's bright lamps emphasized its broad emptiness.
The three men were silent, and, as the driver went past the
street leading to the hotel where Ihsan usually stayed, he
realized submission was his only course.

"I hadn't expected it to be this cold," he remarked, to
hide his confusion. "When I left London, the snow was
already piling up."

None of them said anything. The driver switched on the
heating system to warm the car which, after further silence,
went past the wall surrounding His Highness's mansion and
stopped before its iron back gate, which led to the
reception room and the private guest rooms. On seeing
them, a guard opened the heavy gate. Then they stopped
once more, before the suite annexed to the mansion.

Ihsan couldn't believe what was happening. After he'd
entered, the *fedewi* locked the door of the suite from the

outside, then his footsteps faded away. Ihsan walked around, checking various doors, and found them all locked and keyless. Could they imprison you for no reason? What had His Highness heard, he wondered, to make him angry? Was it Rashid? And what about that donkey of a *fedewi*? But he just carries out orders. Don't get ahead of yourself. Finally tired of speculating, he sank onto the comfortable sofa to wait submissively, but his doze was mingled with a confused apprehension.

At seven in the morning they brought his breakfast on a rosewood trolley covered with a beautiful cloth, drawn in by a waiter. A servant followed and handed Ihsan a copy of the sole newspaper published in Barqais, then hurried to the bedroom and came out again, disappointed to find Ihsan hadn't used it.

"Would you like coffee or tea?" he asked.

They were the first words spoken to him since he'd arrived. He smiled encouragingly, then asked: "Is His Highness in his gathering?"

"I don't know."

"You mean you haven't seen him today? Is he in Barqais?"

"I only concern myself with matters in the kitchen."

It was a dry, blunt answer. Before he left, he asked: "Is there anything else you require, sir?"

"No, thank you."

The two left together, locking the door behind them.

Ihsan drank his coffee, picked at the food, then took a hot shower in the grand bathroom, using some scent from one of the many bottles on the shelf. Time passed slowly and heavily. He read the whole of the newspaper, even the advertisements. Several times he picked up the receiver of the phone, only to lay it down again. You have to be patient,

Ibn Natour, he thought. Don't be so anxious.

At noon, they brought his lunch. The appetizing smells wafted from the various dishes, stirring his hunger. The waiter served him with care until he was full, while the servant cleaned the bathroom. Then the waiter hastily collected up the plates, and the two men left, once more locking the door behind them.

What's happening, he thought, is like some fierce wave surging up from the calmness of the sea, one you can't possibly fight. Just surrender and see where it flings you. You'll know then whether things around you are going to hold or fall apart. But why do you feel this dizziness urging you to submit to whatever might happen, while you wait for it without either longing or fear? The dizziness turns your head and everything around you, so you stop thinking—a slow numbness, without pain or desire, flows suddenly into your veins. You're like a man lost on the surface of a placid sea, but with threatening mouths lurking unseen—a savage shark, opening its jaws beneath the calm expanse, or some fierce, unthought of wave. A strange numbness urges you to surrender, insinuates that resistance, in this moment of awe and apprehension, is useless. And so you let it overwhelm you, let it fill everything around you with a nothingness that makes you say "to hell with it." And then you become quite submissive, with a fondness even for the idea that you're finished.

He dialed Rashid's office number, and got no reply. He tried his home with the same result. When he called Faris, though, the voice came to him, happy and welcoming. After brief preliminaries, Faris asked: "Are you in Barqais, Ihsan?"

"No. In London."

It puzzled him Faris knew nothing of the matter, for

there were very few secrets in Barqais. What's talked of in gatherings and offices makes the rounds through servants, private guards and petty clerks. Faris himself had plenty of spies, but he didn't even know Ihsan was in town!

After the afternoon prayer His Highness came to see him, while the *fedewi* stood behind the door. The man entered with a lofty air, his cane preceding him. For all his frowning countenance, he seemed younger, with newly dyed beard and mustache. His clothes smelled of incense, then, as he reached Ihsan, of a French perfume. Ihsan kept his hand extended until His Highness coolly shook it.

The man sat down on the edge of the sofa, without asking Ihsan to do the same, then exclaimed: "You've blackened my face in front of the Shyoukh, Ihsan. May God blacken yours! That I, at my age, should have had to justify myself to the Shyoukh! You lied to me! Why didn't you tell me it was Ibn al-Ghamry who paved the way for your agreement? The Shyoukh, may God lengthen his life, has been most generous with us. You know what he's done for me, down to the smallest thing. And what's more, Ihsan, I've been good to you, grudged you nothing. All my life I've been honest and trustworthy in my dealings with the Shyoukh. I've never lied to him or cheated him. And now you come to blacken my face! Why didn't you tell me you'd agreed on a commission with al-Ghamry?"

"I never promised him anything."

"You're lying, Ihsan."

He started tapping the floor with his wooden cane.

"Now look, Ihsan. A clear beginning leads to a clear end— that's one of your sayings. Al-Ghamry's due right will be met from your commission. I've promised the Shyoukh that. People can never get enough, can they? Their greed's a bottomless pit! Weren't you satisfied with what I did for you?"

His lips were flecked with foam, his face congested by an anger that reddened his eyes. Ihsan reflected. Surely, he thought, the business of al-Ghamry's commission wouldn't have made him as furious as this. Has he uncovered something else? Is he imprisoning you in his house for the sake of what's due to al-Ghamry? You have to be sure.

"Ibn al-Ghamry did nothing, Your Highness. We started the negotiations from scratch. The men he'd been depending on were worthless—they had nothing to offer us. Hamed al-Ghamry deserves nothing. If they'd really done something, I would never have grudged them their due, and I would have told you about it."

The man's face darkened.

"You don't seem to understand. Commerce has its rules—etiquette—ethics. You'll pay the man his due, Ihsan, whether you like it or not!"

Ihsan realized further resistance was impossible.

"Whatever you say, sir. But don't be angry. All the world's wealth isn't worth your anger."

"All right, sit down. Sit down and write two checks on your accounts. Half a million dollars to Hamed al-Ghamry."

"That's too much, Your Highness!"

"Be quiet! And another half a million dollars to Abdulrahman al-Hemli."

He leaned back, pointing his cane at Ihsan.

"Sit down—write the two checks. I'll hand them to the Shyoukh in the morning. I promised him I'd see they had their due."

His Highness put the checks in his pocket, slammed the door and locked Ihsan in.

Everything around him was very calm, in contrast to his

agitated state. He looked about, seeking some reason for his agitation. He switched on the radio, and the various broadcasting stations reported a calm, monotonous world. He switched it off and turned on the television, which was showing a program about agriculture in Barqais. He cursed the commentator for his overblown description of the gardens, as the camera took endless, trivial close-ups.

Only at dawn was Ihsan able to sleep. On waking, he took a hot shower, dressed and settled down to wait. Some time after he'd had his breakfast, His Highness came in to him, while two guards stood by the door.

"Give me your Barqaisi passport, Ihsan."

Ihsan immediately handed it to him. His Highness gazed at it, with its diplomatic status, and shook his head sadly. Then he produced another passport, which he handed to Ihsan. Stamped on one of its pages, to Ihsan's shocked surprise, were the words: "Valid for one visit only."

"Why this, Your Highness?" he asked.

"Orders from the highest level. From the Shyoukh."

"But I haven't done anything wrong. Quite the reverse. I've been loyal to you. If you'd only permit me to see the Shyoukh, I'll explain things to him."

"Leave things to me. It's simpler that way, God willing. He'll change his mind when he calms down, but for the moment we have to carry out his orders. Leave the country now. Then we'll see."

The irony in the voice did nothing to dispel Ihsan's qualms. The two guards stayed with him until the plane took off. He felt a deep and utter sense of dejection as Barqais faded gradually into the distance through the plane's window.

The threads of rain bound the darkened London sky to streets swallowing the water down its gutters, and lightning flashed several times through the taxi window. The raindrops beat on the roof of the car, pounding in his head like the beating of drums. Ihsan pulled back the glass partition and spoke to the driver.

"When did this rain start?"

"Yesterday. According to the forecast, it won't stop before tomorrow."

It rains summer and winter here, he thought, and everything turns green. Water revives the lives of plants and other things. There the blazing sun burns everything, but divine wisdom revives life's drought, with a black rain bursting up from the bowels of the earth, spreading its bounty over the arid desert, and then that turns green. Divine wisdom, Ihsan. Divine wisdom!

When he reached his door, the driver emerged with the suitcase, his clothes getting drenched from the rain.

"You should have told me you didn't have any change, sir," he said angrily, "before you hired me."

Ihsan handed him the fifty-pound note.

"Keep the change," he said.

"I'm sorry, sir?"

Ihsan's personal driver rushed forward with an open umbrella, and the porter hurried to carry his suitcase. The taxi driver just stared at the rich man he'd brought home.

Ihsan went to the phone and dialed a number.

"Jessica. Where's Nadia?"

"I don't know. I haven't seen her for two days."

No one else knew where she was either. Ihsan searched

everywhere for her. Then he got frightened, started shouting and almost called the police before deciding, finally, to wait until morning.

She turned up at noon, looking elegant and haughty despite the sadness in her eyes.

"Where have you been?" he cried, relieved.

"Why should you care?"

"Nadia!"

She gave a contemptuous shrug, then added, as she moved upstairs: "You go away for weeks without telling me where you are. I've been away for just three days—in fifteen years of marriage."

He ran after her, panic-stricken. Clutching her arm, he pulled her back down the two stairs she'd climbed.

"This is no joking matter, Nadia. Where have you been?"

"What's the matter with you, Ihsan Natour? Did you buy me once long ago, then forget about me?"

"Where have you been? Who with?"

She broke away, her eyes wide with fury and resentment.

"How dare you imagine such a thing, Ibn Natour! Is that how sick your mind is? I won't act the way you have, Ihsan. It's not for your sake I keep myself clean; it's out of respect for my own humanity, because I refuse to be anyone's object of enjoyment. I'm doing it for my sake, not yours."

His face relaxed a little. But she hadn't finished.

"How dare you imagine you can drop me wherever you like, and expect me just to stand there, waiting for you to come and pick me up again when you happen to feel like it! To get myself ready for your arrival, when I don't even know where you are? You thought you were the axis and I'd go on and on revolving around you. Even the heavenly bodies break from their spheres sometimes. Didn't you know that? They burn, maybe, but they're free."

She took a small envelope from her handbag, and two photos fluttered out. The first fell face down on the table. The second fell on the silk rug; he was embracing Angela, both of them in bathing suits.

He stood there for some moments, speechless.

"Where did you get those?"

"It doesn't matter where I got them or how I found out. The important thing is that I paid half a million dollars for them!"

"Who to?"

"To Rashid Salman—I met him and Angela. You didn't realize, I suppose, that she'd been his mistress, then the mistress of His Highness's son, before she became yours?"

"He's lying. It's a lie!"

She turned the first photo face up and flung it at him.

"How about this? Is this a lie too?"

There was Angela, kissing him lovingly. He sank down, unable to take any more.

"Where did you see Rashid Salman?"

"In Geneva. He asked to see me there. I've sorted things out with him and Angela—yes, with Angela, who sold you for a quarter of a million dollars. We haggled over you!"

"Angela?"

"Oh, she's beautiful, no doubt. But Angela's like you. You're both from the same mold, which is why you couldn't see what she was really like. Or that she'd cooked it all up with Rashid Salman. She was the bait he used to catch you."

"The dog! The pimp! Why did he do it? I never did him any harm."

"You informed on him to His Highness. He had to leave Barqais."

"Rashid Salman?"

"Didn't you know that? His Highness's son was removed from his post, and Rashid left Barqais on the first plane afterwards."

"But I didn't inform on him. We both fell in the same trap!"

"They seized his moneys in Barqais, asked for his accounts in European banks to be frozen, then put him in prison. But he managed to stop all that by sending a single letter."

"Who to?"

"To His Highness. He threatened to publish certain documents and photographs no one would want to see the light of day. He said that if they touched his money, he'd publish them in every newspaper in the world. They gave in to him, but he was expelled from Barqais. I had to buy his silence. Not for your sake, Ihsan, but to preserve my dignity and your image in front of the children."

Ihsan was speechless. The situation was bigger than any cunning he was capable of. The decision, he knew, was hers alone now.

NOTES

[1] *Ustadh*: A teacher, a university professor, a learned man. It is sometimes used, as here, in personal address.

[2] *Dashdasha*: A long, wide robe worn in the Gulf region.

[3] Throughout the novel this character (whose personal name is not given) is referred to and addressed by the formula *tawil al-'umr* (may he/you live long), indicative of his noble rank. This translation henceforth renders the formula simply as "His Highness" (or "Your Highness" in personal address).

[4] *Rakwa*: An eastern type of coffee brewer.

[5] Ibn Natour: Son of Natour.

[6] *Shyoukh*: The colloquial Gulf pronunciation of *shuyoukh*, the plural of *shaykh* (sheikh). The plural is commonly used in this way, in referring to a person, to indicate esteem and reverence.

[7] The reference is to Ghassan Kanafani's famous novel *Men in the Sun* (published 1962), which describes how three Palestinian men seeking work die in a desperate attempt to have themselves smuggled into a Gulf state.

[8] The Arabic here consists of pious formulae. *Salli annabi*: Pray upon the Prophet. *Allahoma salli ala sayidina Muhammad*: May God pray upon our Master Muhammad. *Uthkor Allah*: Obey the commands of God. *Wanima billah*: God is our blessed refuge.

[9] *Fedewi*: A kind of personal bodyguard, employed in a sheikh's house in the Gulf region.

[10] *Nargila*: A kind of pipe in which the tobacco is drawn through water.

[11] Women in many Arab countries are commonly referred to as "Um" (mother of) followed by the name of the eldest son (or eldest daughter if there is no son). The male equivalent is "Abu."

[12] The reference is to the main character in Níkos Kazantzakís's novel *Zorba the Greek* (published 1946).

[13] *Zahrat al-Mada'in*: The Rose of Cities (meaning Jerusalem).

[14] Foster mother organization: An organization for fostering the children of martyrs.

[15] Muawiya (d. 680 AD) was an early caliph and founder of the Umayyad dynasty in Damascus. The reference is to his saying: "If there were a hair between me and the people, I would not allow it to be severed. I would slacken it when they drew, and draw it when they slackened."